I'M WITH YOU

THE ASPEN SERIES

CINDY STARK

OLIVERHEBERBOOKS

Published by Oliver-Heber Books

0 9 8 7 6 5 4 3 2 1

 Created with Vellum

1

Zoe Cassidy glanced down each aisle of Randall's Western Outfitters as she walked around the country store, searching for packing tape. Mr. Randall had an odd way of categorizing items. Power tools hung next to women's socks, and apparently, adhesives and toilet plungers belonged together. The citizens of Aspen often joked about his system, but Zoe suspected it was Mr. Randall's way of keeping people in the store longer, hoping they'd buy more stuff.

"Ha," Zoe muttered when she spied the adhesives and turned her cart in that direction. If the day went according to plan, she'd have everything except her big furniture moved into her new, turn-of-the-century house by evening. Finally, a place she could call home, a luxury she'd never enjoyed until now.

She was halfway down the aisle when Asher Campbell entered from the opposite way, and she screeched to a halt.

Why?

She asked the same question each time she had the unfortunate experience of running into him. In a town as small as Aspen, she should probably consider herself lucky that she didn't bump into him more often. But every time she did...ugh.

She might have gotten over past hurts and her damned attraction to him if he'd gone bald or gained a gut during the ten years since high school, but he hadn't. If anything, he looked better. Ripped jeans showcased powerful thighs. Dark hair peeked from beneath a dusty ball cap. His broad shoulders could certainly carry the weight of the world if he wanted.

And those eyes. Those stormy gray eyes that peeked from beneath his lashes when he'd watched her. He was probably dreaming up the next awful remark he'd say to her.

Didn't matter. He didn't matter. She was beyond that era of her life. She'd get her tape and leave. No need to speak a word to the obnoxious man.

The moment she moved faster down the aisle, he glanced up.

She quickly shifted her gaze as though she hadn't noticed him and focused on her targeted supplies. But out of the corner of her eye, she caught him striding purposefully toward her.

Why couldn't he leave her alone?

Their carts nearly collided as they both stopped in front of the packing tape. "Afternoon, Zoe. Long time, no see."

Even his voice was sexy with deep resonating sounds that affected her more than she cared to admit. She truly hated him.

With a quick glance in his direction, she acknowledged his presence. She couldn't find anything nice to say, so she said nothing at all. Instead, she snatched two rolls of tape and dropped them in her cart.

"Are you finally moving out of Olga's basement?" Asher asked when she didn't answer. "What a dump. I don't know how you stood to live there that long."

She frowned as his insult bored deep into her soul. It wasn't like she'd enjoyed living in a dark hole with an eccentric lady as a landlord. But a single girl, whose mother had taken off to

God-knows-where many years ago, couldn't afford to be too choosy.

Emotional words clawed their way up her throat, and this time she opened her mouth. "Do you always have to be such a jerk?"

He widened his beautiful eyes as though surprised by her remark. "I didn't mean it like that, Zoe."

That's what he always said after insulting her in whatever fashion suited him at the moment. It was like some weird bait and switch routine he used on her. Insult her and then deny it. Not this time.

She tossed her invisible shield between them and curved her lips into a chilled smile. "Have a nice day, Asher."

Then she turned and walked away.

Dammit. She'd sworn the last time she'd encountered him, she wouldn't allow him to push her buttons again. But he'd managed it so easily. Why?

What was it about him that gave him power over her, that allowed him to cut her so easily with careless words?

She shook off her annoyance and focused on the day ahead. She needed to get to her new home and start cleaning. Old Man Jenkins had declined since the death of his wife and hadn't left it in the best state. Which meant she had work to do before she could move in. Still, if she put her frustrations into her work, she'd be too busy and too tired to think of anything or anyone else.

First, she had one more stop to make before she headed home.

Home. Her home.

Yes.

———

"Dammit." Asher watched the one woman who stirred his blood like no other walk away. Why?

Zoe's loose blond curls swayed as she walked with a grace that contradicted her backwoods, redneck upbringing. Even in their younger years, when she'd been all knees and elbows, she'd exuded a natural beauty that he hadn't been able to ignore.

It was unfortunate that she'd turned out to be full of piss and vinegar instead of sugar and spice and everything nice. Not that he could blame her, but...

"I see you're still charming the ladies," Seth Moore said as he approached.

Asher fired a glare at his long-time friend and recent business partner. "Whatever."

Together, they'd started their own business and had currently built nearly a third of the new houses in town that year. He cared far more about that than a sassy woman, no matter how pretty she was.

The blond construction worker chuckled. "You're the only guy I know who's pissed off a woman just by existing."

He turned to Seth. "Right? What the hell is up with that? She's hated me for years, and what did I ever do to her?"

Seth shrugged as he readjusted his ball cap, giving Asher a glimpse of flattened blond hair. "Women. Who can figure them out?"

He pulled a roll of packing tape from the shelf. "Not me. That's for damn sure."

Especially after his ex-wife had kicked him out of their home months ago. She'd needed to make room for the new man in her life, and Asher had been in the way.

He still couldn't quite stomach that.

Thank God, he'd finally found somewhere to live. Luckily,

he wouldn't need to pack much since most of his stuff was still in boxes.

His friend tested the weight of the hammer he carried. "Honestly, I'm not sure why you care. If Zoe can't be nice, who needs her?"

Asher stared at his friend, letting his words drill home. "You're right. I've tried to be friendly. If she can't do the same, something's wrong with her."

Even as he said it, he regretted it. He'd known of her struggles through childhood. He'd admired the strength she'd shown when others had made fun of her because her clothes were outdated. Or when she was late because her mom had been too wasted to drive her to school. She'd let the teasing roll right off her back and get on with whatever she'd been doing.

He scrubbed the short whiskers on his chin, remembering the many times he'd fought hard to gain enough courage to talk to the elusive, quiet blond beauty, to tell her what he thought of her. But his tongue had always tripped him up and he'd say some stupid shit like he had just now. Then she'd leave him standing like a lone fool.

Different variations of the scenarios played through his head, all with the same outcome. Maybe he'd never understand women, as evidenced by his recent divorce. Really, what the hell did he care about any of them?

"What time do you want me to show up in the morning to help move your stuff?" Seth asked.

Asher had been camping in his friend Milo's spare room for the past few months, but he'd grown tired of intruding on him, his wife, and their new baby. When an old friend of his mom's mentioned he'd thought of selling his place, Asher had been all over that. It would be quiet and on the outskirts of town. The perfect place to mend a broken heart.

He jutted his chin at Seth. "About seven-thirty? Eight?"

Seth lifted his chin in a decisive nod. "You got it, buddy. By the way, I saw Dana the other day. She wanted me to ask you to back off on making her pay you for your share of the equity in the house."

Anger scratched at him like a bare tree branch in a windstorm, constant and annoying. "What did you say?"

"I told her it wasn't my business, and I wouldn't get involved."

Asher paused and then nodded. "Thanks, man."

The thought of his ex-wife and their messy divorce was still a potent source of pain for him, and any mention was a cattle prod in an open wound.

He'd aired the dirty trash left over from his marriage to Seth and Milo many times over too many beers. Thankfully, they'd supported him like brothers.

After a time, he'd realized he could bitch about his circumstances all he wanted, but it wouldn't change anything. What was done, was done. Continuing to talk about and dwell on how badly Dana had treated him only served to bleed his pain and prevent his heart from healing.

Seth clapped him on the shoulder. "Hang in there. Having your own place will make it better. You can work on fixing up the old house when you want, and sit around in your boxers all day and drink beer when you don't, and no one will say a word."

A semblance of a smile hit his lips. "Yeah." There was that to look forward to.

2

Zoe tossed the moving boxes into the trunk of her blue Mazda and slammed it shut. Then she took a quick glance over her shoulder to make sure Asher hadn't followed her out of the store. She had one more very important stop before she headed home to pack the last of her meager things, and she didn't want him following her there.

The coast was clear, so she left her car where it was and dashed toward Rumors Coffee Shop. The bell on the door tinkled as she entered, and the exquisite scent of delicious cinnamon rolls surrounded her like a comforting hug.

Noelle Parker looked up, her blond ponytail sliding over her shoulder as a bright smile lit her face. "About time," she scolded.

"You know," Zoe said as she approached the counter. "I'll have to stop coming in every day now that I have a mortgage to pay."

"Uh-huh." Noelle's grin grew bigger. "Your usual, then?"

She nodded, her own smile growing. "I mean it. Your cinnamon rolls are the devil on my waistline and my pocketbook."

"Yeah, but we both know you can't resist." Noelle passed a plate of sinful goodness toward her, and Zoe groaned.

"Ugh. You're right. I'm so totally addicted to these things that it isn't funny." She pulled a corner off the roll, slid it into her mouth, and savored the bite. "So unbelievably good."

"Coffee, too?" Noelle asked.

"Of course." Zoe slid her money across the counter, picked up her cinnamon roll and headed for the nearest empty table. Every day, it seemed more and more customers filled the cozy shop, and Zoe couldn't be happier about her friend's success.

Noelle joined her a few moments later, as was customary, carrying two cups of coffee. She sat and slid one to Zoe. "How goes the packing? Are you about ready to move?"

"I just picked up a few more empty boxes," she said around a mouthful. "I'm going over after this to clean. Thanks again for asking Kade to move my bed and the kitchen table. I don't know what I'd do without you guys." She'd learned to treasure her dear friends as though they were family. Hell, they *were* her family.

Noelle finished her sip of coffee and then nodded. "Of course. You know Kade. He's always happy to help anyone in need."

Zoe licked the frosting from her finger, relishing the creamy vanilla flavor. "You're so lucky. I think you picked the last decent guy in Aspen."

"You sound like me this time last year," Noelle said with a shake of her head. "I swore I'd never find anyone, and then Kade came into my life and *bam*. Nothing's been the same since."

"Right? I mean, look at you. You're happier than the yellow walls you have in here. It's disgusting." Her friend practically spilled joy all around her like fairy dust, and it was hard not to be ecstatic for her and jealous at the same time.

Noelle tilted her head with a huge smile on her face. "It is pretty amazing."

"Of course it is. On the other hand, we could talk about my life, where the most exciting thing that happened to me today was that I was unlucky enough to run into Asher Campbell. And you know he can't pass up the opportunity to insult me. *Or...*we could talk about you and the wedding."

"Come on, Zoe. Asher's not that bad. I've been around him tons of times, and he's always been nice to me."

She narrowed her gaze in jest, warning her friend that she'd trampled into dangerous territory. "He pushed me in the mud, Noelle."

"When you were five," she volleyed back.

"What about prom?" Asher had let everyone know he'd intended to invite her. She'd given him a chance then, was even excited to go. But then he'd invited Emily instead, asking her right in front of Zoe. Everyone knew, and she'd been beyond humiliated.

"That was high school. Really, Zoe, he's a good guy."

Why did everyone always feel the need to defend him? Couldn't they see how he was? She folded her arms across her chest in a protective gesture, no longer wanting to continue this vein of conversation. "Look, I know you all like him, but I can't ignore what he's said to me. For some reason, he doesn't like me, so I'm not going to try to like him. I don't have time for people like that in my life."

Noelle shook her head in disagreement. "I wish you could see the guy I see. The other day, I saw him carrying Betty Johnson's groceries out to the car for her."

"Not going to happen. He's a jerk to me on his best days, an asshole on all the rest. Don't try to make me think otherwise, because I've seen the dark side of him and that's enough." She pulled off a large bite of roll and stuffed it into her mouth.

Noelle frowned.

"Why do you care if I like him or not?" she said, her words muffled by the cinnamon roll. Her friend's insistence was like a pesky fly she wanted to swat once and for all.

Her friend shrugged. "I don't know. I like him, and I keep thinking you must be missing something the rest of us see."

"The more of him I miss, the better." Zoe swallowed and inhaled a deep, cleansing breath. "Wedding. I want wedding news."

For a moment, Noelle acted as though she'd continue debating her point, but then seemed to think better of it. "*Ten weeks*. I can hardly believe it."

Zoe either. At the end of that short amount of time, Noelle would be the last of her friends to get married, with no viable prospects on the horizon for herself. "I'm totally throwing you a pre-wedding party as soon as I'm settled in the house. Maybe I'll do a barbeque. Invite the guys, too."

The more people, the merrier. She would keep so busy that she wouldn't have time to think about her forever-alone status.

Noelle stood and leaned over the table to hug her. "Really? That's so sweet of you."

She grinned. "You deserve all the sweet things in life."

———

Hours later, Zoe groaned as she straightened her aching back. "*Ugh*."

Her new kitchen was now spotless after scrubbing every inch, followed by unpacking boxes and organizing cupboards and drawers. It had taken her nearly the whole day to get her house in a habitable state and to bring in most everything she owned.

It was worth it, though. The country kitchen was larger

than many she'd seen. The warm woods glowed with charm, and the large picture window showcased the beautiful, wild hills behind her house. She would love sitting there every morning watching the seasons change.

She needed curtains, though, for the smaller window above the sink. Maybe some pretty lace ones that would befit a home built in the early 1900s. She liked that about her place. It had character and stamina and history. Much better than all those new, bland houses Asher built.

She was sad for Old Man Jenkins, certain he would miss living in the house. He'd been happily married until a few years ago when his wife had up and died unexpectedly from a stroke.

He'd decided to sell before he got too old, but Zoe wondered if it was already too late for that. Sometimes, his mind would wander, and he'd go off on tangents about random things. Still, he'd said he had a bucket list he needed to attend to, and who was she to argue? He no longer wanted his home, and she loved it.

She stepped into the living room and pulled her antique lamp from the box and set it on the small table near the window. It was perfect for her house, and would be right next to where she'd place her chair when it arrived. Each day, she'd watch the sun set fire to the sky over the green fields beyond her house as it settled for the night.

Asher had been right about one thing. Her apartment had been a dismal place that she'd barely tolerated. Still, he didn't need to rub it in her face.

She twisted the knob on the lamp to chase away the night. Instead of light, a loud pop ricocheted off the walls. She stumbled back in surprise as everything went dark. In her haste to retreat, she lost her footing and landed hard on her butt. "Shit," she whispered and then released a soft laugh, embarrassed that she'd fallen.

One light in the kitchen remained illuminated, casting creepy shadows around the room. She got to her feet and twisted the knob on the lamp again. Dead. The lamp must have tripped a breaker. Hopefully, that wouldn't be a common occurrence.

But it wasn't the end of the world.

She wouldn't go hunting for the breaker box that night, not with a good portion of the unfamiliar house in darkness. She'd find it tomorrow, flip the tripped switch, and all would be good. Until then, she had light from the kitchen and candles if she needed them.

It was time to call it a night, anyway. She could finish the rest tomorrow morning after Kade brought her furniture.

Of course, that meant she wouldn't have her bed until then, either. But she'd already decided to sleep on the floor instead of returning to her apartment. The hard surface would be worth staying in her own place. She had her own slice of heaven now, and she never intended to leave.

Also, her new home had a lovely, oversized claw-foot tub that was available and ready for immediate use. She wasn't about to pass up that luxury.

She quickly secured her car in the small attached garage, locked the front door to the house, and headed toward the stairs. Unfortunately, the lights weren't working on the second floor either, so she returned to the kitchen and retrieved the candles she'd unpacked earlier in the day.

Flickering candlelight danced over the walls in the bathroom as she turned on the faucet. While the tub filled, she unpacked shampoo, soap, and bubble bath.

Her antique, exquisite tub deserved bubbles, and so did she. Her muscles would thank her for a soak in hot water, and she needed them to be appreciative before they realized they weren't getting a soft bed to sleep on that night.

Asher backed his truck into the drive of his new home, grateful to be away from the crying baby. Kiley was adorable and all that, but she'd picked up on the minor squabble her parents had when Milo had stopped by for dinner during his shift. They both had plenty to say about whose turn it was to get up at the four a.m. feeding, and the baby let it be known she wasn't happy.

Milo and Anna had never made him feel like he was in the way, but that's exactly what he was. What couple wanted an extra guy hanging around while they adjusted to their expanded family?

He sure as hell wouldn't.

When he'd told them at dinner that he'd planned to move his new mattress from the barn, where he'd stored it along with other things, they hadn't argued with him even though the hour was late and everything could have waited until morning. They needed their space, and he needed his.

Asher jumped from the cab of his truck and headed for the front door. Already things felt calmer. He'd scoped out the house a few days ago, chosen the larger bedroom for sleeping and the smaller for an office and storage space. The living room was large enough for his couch and big screen TV, and he hoped his ex enjoyed sitting on the floor and watching nothing.

Except she and the jerk who'd moved in with her probably had better things to do.

"Dammit," he whispered as he pulled the house key from his pocket. He had to stop thinking about her, about what he might have done differently that could have prevented their divorce, about what she was doing now. She'd wanted out, and he'd given it to her. What was done was done, and it was time to move on.

He opened the door, surprised to find a light on in the back of the house. Maybe Jenkins had forgotten to turn it off. Looked like he'd left a few pieces of unwanted furniture, too. Then again, the old man had a few screws loose.

Still, with the great deal he'd gotten on the place, he could handle whatever came his way.

Asher entered the kitchen, noticed a few packing boxes on the floor and a big cinnamon roll from Rumors tempting him from the counter.

Had Seth and April already stopped by? It would be like April to bring him a welcome gift from the shop she ran with Noelle.

Weird that Milo hadn't mentioned anything about Seth showing up early to haul boxes for him, but he and Anna had been well into their dispute when Asher had gotten home. Either way, it was a pleasant surprise.

He lifted the lid, pulled out the pastry, and shoved a big chunk of it into his mouth. *Damn.* So good. He leaned against the counter and relaxed into his thoughts. The house was great. A nice place, really.

He could heal here. Start again. Make a better life.

This time around, he'd take things slower and not rush into anything like he had with Dana. He'd protect his heart and his assets. Love might be some grand thing, but it could also be a cold-hearted bitch when things went south.

The sound of water running through the pipes in the house caught his attention, and he jerked around in surprise, wondering if Seth and April were still there.

3

Asher had climbed half the stairs, heading toward the bathroom, before he remembered there had been no other cars outside. It occurred to him that someone might have broken in, and he contemplated returning to his truck. He kept a pistol in the glove compartment, and it might be wise to have it before he interrupted whoever was in his house.

But then the sound of a woman singing decided for him. The only logical explanation was that Seth must have dropped off April and returned for another load. He and Asher had probably passed each other on the road, and he'd been so caught up in his thoughts that he hadn't noticed.

Asher continued up the stairs, following the sound of her voice, ready to thank April for all her help. Flickering light beckoned from the bathroom, and the water turned off abruptly as he reached the doorway.

"Hello? April?" he called as he entered the room.

A woman screamed, startling him.

"Shit!" he yelled in response, unable to look away from a naked Zoe Cassidy in his tub.

She splashed, trying to cover herself, and he quickly realized staring any longer would result in severe repercussions. He stumbled into the hall, still half dazed.

"What the hell are you doing, Zoe?" He couldn't keep the shock from his voice. She was there. Naked. In his tub.

"Get out!" Zoe's shrill voice shook with rage. "Get the hell out of my house right now, Asher!"

Her words lit a fuse inside him, forcing him to defend his actions. "*Your house*? Excuse me. This is *my house*." Like she had a right to get indignant and make demands. Forgoing his manners as she'd done, he stepped back into the room to find she'd sunk to her chin in bubbles.

She shook her head vehemently as fiery sparks blasted from her eyes. "This is my house. I purchased it from Bob Jenkins last week. Now get the hell out!"

He moved farther into the room until he towered over her. He jabbed his thumb against his chest. "*I* bought it from Jenkins. I have a bill of sale to prove it."

"Show me," she demanded.

He scoffed. "I don't have it on me, for hell's sake."

"You're lying." She grabbed for the towel next to the tub. "Turn around. No. Get out. Just get the hell out."

With a breath of heated frustration, he left the room before he upset her further. Best thing he could do was get the papers from his truck, prove his rights, and then see what she had to say for herself. Fighting with an emotional woman without proper ammunition wouldn't help him in the least. He'd learned that lesson the hard way.

———

When Zoe stood, her legs shook from the overdose of adrenaline spiking her veins from Asher barging into her bathroom. Breaking and entering had to be a felony crime. Scaring the shit out of her should be another.

She wrapped a large towel around her and stepped from the tub. What the hell could he be thinking, trespassing like that? Was this some kind of joke? She couldn't come up with a reason for his intrusion unless he'd snapped mentally and, for whatever reason, had zeroed in on her.

Or maybe his target had been Jenkins, because how would Asher even know she'd purchased the house? She'd told very few people. Granted, Aspen was a small town, but her news didn't rise to the level of salacious gossip.

She didn't know if she was in danger at this point or not, but he'd caught her in the most vulnerable position possible, and she needed to rectify that immediately.

She slipped the towel around her and gripped the edges as she slowly stepped into the hall. As she did, the sound of the front door closing echoed through the quiet house.

"Asher?" she called, trying to figure out if he'd left or not.

No response.

Leaving a trail of wet footprints, she hurried down the stairs and peeked through the front window in time to see Asher open his passenger door.

Perfect. She dashed to the front door and twisted the lock. She was certain she'd done the same before she'd called it a night, but she'd obviously forgotten or hadn't shut the door tight enough.

She quickly made her way into the kitchen for her cell phone. There, on the counter next to her keys, lay the empty plastic container that had once housed her cinnamon roll.

"*Son of a bitch.*" He would pay for that.

She clenched her jaw and dialed the county's emergency number on her phone and gave the dispatcher her address. "I need to report a break in. The man's name is Asher Campbell.

He's still here, but he's now outside. Please send someone as soon as possible."

"Are you hurt or in danger of being hurt, ma'am?" the dispatcher asked.

She hesitated for a moment. She wanted to say yes, but the only thing he'd damaged so far was her cinnamon roll. "I don't think so, though he might be having a mental breakdown. He thinks he owns my house."

"Okay, ma'am. I'm sending an officer to your location. Would you like me to stay on the line with you until he arrives?"

"No. I think I'm okay. I've locked the door." Plus, she needed to get dressed before the officers arrived.

"Yes, ma'am. Call back if the situation changes." The dispatcher hung up, and Zoe turned, intending to head upstairs and get dressed.

But there was Asher standing in front of her, and she screamed again as her heart bottomed out.

"*Shit.*" Asher held up his hands. "Will you stop that? You're freaking me out."

Zoe's heart thundered in her chest. "*How did you get in here? I locked that door.*" Unless the lock was defective. Perhaps she should have kept the dispatcher on the phone after all.

Asher slapped a key on the counter. "I told you. It's my house."

She stared at the key as her mind ravaged through possibilities like a raccoon in open trash. "No. It's *my* house. I just bought it."

He thrust several papers toward her.

Fear snuck up on her and sent her emotions curling into a ball. "What are those?"

Triumph danced in his eyes. "The handwritten bill of sale to this house that you're claiming is yours."

She clutched the towel against her chest while she took the

papers from him. This had to be a scam. There was no other explanation.

As she scanned the words on the documents, her insides tangled into unbearable knots.

It appeared Jenkins had also sold his house to Asher. Unless… "You forged this. I don't know how or why you'd do such a thing, but there's no way Mr. Jenkins would have sold it to both of us."

Asher narrowed his gaze. "I guess that remains to be seen. I've shown my proof. I've yet to see yours." He scanned her up and down, leaving a trail of shivers in his wake.

She needed a minute to think. To breathe. "I'm getting dressed. Then I'll get my proof. The cops will be here soon, and we'll see what they have to say about the whole thing."

"You called the police?" He seemed genuinely surprised by her actions. Maybe the threat of their arrival would scare him off.

"If you don't want to be in trouble, you might want to leave now."

He shrugged his shoulders and gave her a nonchalant smile. "Doesn't bother me at all. I have nothing to hide. Might be best to let them handle the matter."

She frowned, not happy with his response. "Fine. Let them handle it." She left the kitchen with fear and frustration chasing behind her.

"What's wrong with the lights?" he hollered.

She didn't bother answering.

She was in the right. So Asher had to be wrong. The police would sense that immediately, right? She had valid documents, signed papers that proved her ownership.

God, this was insane. She'd never liked Asher. But he had seemed sane.

Still, what other explanation could there be?

4

Zoe didn't leave her room when the lights suddenly came on. Asher must have fixed the breaker, but that wasn't enough to draw her out. She remained locked in her bedroom until she spotted red and blue lights flashing in her front yard.

As soon as she did, she snatched the packet that held her mortgage papers and cracked opened her door. The hallway was empty.

With her heart thundering, she hurried to the stairs and then down to the seemingly unoccupied first floor.

Maybe Asher had taken her advice and left.

She flung open the front door to find red and blue lights reflecting off the pines and aspens in her front yard. Asher stood near the bottom of the porch stairs with Deputy Milo Sykes. The blond officer nodded as Asher spoke.

"I walk in my house, and there she is in my tub. Then she starts freaking out and yelling at me—"

"Hey!" Zoe hurried down the stairs, papers in hand. "Don't be telling him lies. This is my house, my tub."

Milo held up two hands. "Whoa, now, both of you." He shot

a glance at Zoe. "Let him finish, and then you'll get your turn to speak."

Zoe bit her tongue and shook her head vehemently in response to Asher's account of recent events.

"So, I don't know where the hell she's coming from," Asher said as he finished. "But this house clearly belongs to me. You know this, Milo. Hell, you watched me go through the process."

Deputy Sykes nodded. "I did."

"No." Zoe thrust her mortgage packet toward the officer. "I don't know what house he thinks he bought, but this one is mine. Mr. Jenkins' signature is on the paperwork, and the key he gave me fits the lock. *Mine.* Check with Betty Johnson. She handled the sale."

"My key fits that lock, too," Asher said with a look of defiance.

If she lost her house now, she'd be homeless, since Olga already had someone new waiting to move in. She twisted her fingers together to keep them from shaking. "Then you stole it."

"Let's take this inside," Milo said. "I need better lighting to review these documents."

Zoe walked past Asher like he was a coiled rattler as he held the front door open for her.

The three of them reconvened in the kitchen, where Deputy Sykes spread out the paperwork on the counter. Asher looked over his shoulder and a frown settled on his forehead.

After a few moments, Milo turned to both of them with a puzzled look. "I'll admit this is quite the conundrum. It appears Jenkins has sold his property to both of you."

"*What?*" they both said in unison.

"He wouldn't," Zoe said.

"He can't do that," Asher added.

"We'll need to contact him to sort this out. Do either of you have a phone number where I can reach him?" Milo asked.

Sick apprehension slithered through Zoe as she shook her head. "He said something about Tahiti, but I didn't really believe him."

"*Shit*," Asher hissed. "If he's somewhere spending my money, and I don't get this house, I'll kill him."

Zoe raised her brows. "Not a smart thing to admit to a cop."

He narrowed his gaze at her. "Milo knows me well enough to know I'm kidding."

"I'm going to need your paperwork, both of you," Milo said. "You can either let me take the originals or bring me copies tomorrow so I can begin the investigation. I'll do what I can to search for Jenkins tonight."

Zoe glanced between him and Asher. "What do we do in the meantime? I already have stuff moved in. Tomorrow's the last day I'll have my apartment, and I don't have anywhere else to stay."

"I don't either," Asher countered and focused on her. "Why can't you let your landlord know you need your place longer?"

"Why don't you?" she tossed back at him, irritated that he thought his concerns were more important.

"I am his landlord, so to speak." Milo turned to Asher. "You know you're more than welcome to stay at our house for as long as you need."

Asher shook his head. "We both know I've already over-stayed my welcome. You and Anna need time to bond with your new baby without tripping over me."

Milo's radio crackled, and he paused their conversation to respond to the dispatcher. Then he met their gazes. "Sorry to leave you both in the lurch, but I've got another call. For now, the two of you will need to figure out who stays and who goes until we have more answers. I trust you can both be adults about it and solve it equitably. Toss a coin if you have to."

Despair filled Zoe as Milo left the kitchen. How could her life go from the best day ever to this?

A moment later, the sound of the front door closing echoed through the quiet house. She and Asher both remained where Milo had left them. An awkward silence descended upon them as the sound of Milo's engine disappeared in the distance, leaving them alone.

Zoe lifted her gaze to find Asher staring solemnly at the floor. "You're not going to be a gentleman and offer to let me stay?"

He frowned. "Why is it the guy is always the one who has to be kicked out of his home? Shouldn't the ladies be nice sometimes?"

The anger behind his words left her with nothing to say.

"Look, I'd let you have it, but I have nowhere else to go," Asher said after a few moments. "Their baby cries incessantly, and I'll lose my mind if I have to listen to her any longer. If you want, I'll see if they'll let *you* stay with them."

She drew her brows in defiance and folded her arms. "I'm not leaving." This was *her* house, her supposed sanctuary, and she couldn't give it up so easily.

"I'm not either," he said and straightened. "I have just as much ownership as you do at this point, and I need a place to crash. I don't see any reason we can't inhabit the same place for a couple of days until we discover who Jenkins swindled and who owns the house. I sure as hell am not going to rent an apartment in the meantime. If it's too difficult for you to spend a few days under the same roof as me, find another place."

She clenched her jaw and shook her head.

"Good. Then it's settled. Since you already took my bedroom, I'll graciously take the smaller of the two." With that, he strode out of the kitchen and let the door slam as he left the house.

The reality of her situation hit her, and tears forced their way to the surface. She could seriously lose her dream home. Worse, the bank would still expect her to pay on the mortgage unless she could recover the money. She wasn't sure she could afford an apartment after that.

She wasn't a stranger to homelessness, but dammit, she'd sworn it would never happen to her again. Not as long as she could breathe enough to work.

How could Jenkins have done such a thing? She'd known the man most of her life. Not well, maybe, but he had a decent reputation around town.

Her mind taunted her with wild thoughts until she was in danger of completely losing her sanity.

In a desperate attempt to save herself, she lifted her cell and dialed Noelle's number. "I'm sorry for calling so late," Zoe said with a hitch in her voice when her friend answered. "I need someone to talk me down."

"What happened?" Noelle asked, concern in her sleepy voice. "What's wrong?"

Zoe quickly repeated the details between small sobs. She did her best to keep her emotions intact, but a few slipped out.

"What the hell do I do now, Noelle? I may have lost my savings and might have nowhere to live." This couldn't be real. Any moment, she'd wake up and thank God it had all been a nightmare.

"Oh, hell. That's unbelievable, Zoe."

"Asher refuses to leave until he finds out whether it's his house. He thinks we should stay here together. Can you imagine?" She grabbed a tissue and wiped her eyes. "How am I supposed to live with someone I can't stand?"

"Oh, Zoe. I'm so sorry. The entire situation is unreal. I'm sure Kade would let you have a room at the motel."

That would likely work for a day or two, but what if it took longer? "I don't think I should leave. Isn't possession nine-tenths of the law or something like that? If he's here, it might be more likely he'll be the one who gets to stay."

Noelle remained silent for several long moments. "That might be true. But maybe it won't be as bad as you think. Kade and I have spent time with Asher at Milo's house. I know you don't want to hear it, but I like the guy. Maybe you will eventually, too," she said with a hopeful voice.

A weighted sigh escaped her lips, and she closed her eyes. "Please don't say that. Don't make me try to like him. I need you on my side right now."

"I am on your side, Zoe. I'm only saying this about him because I want you to know you'll be okay."

Except she was terrified she wouldn't be. There was an actual possibility that nothing would be okay again. She opened her eyes and blinked rapidly to clear the remaining tears. Talking to Noelle wasn't helping. "I'm going to go now. I can't think about this anymore. I think I need to sleep."

Her friend released a long sigh. "Okay, Zo. Come see me tomorrow. Your cinnamon roll is on me."

"Yeah." About that... She had yet to give Asher a piece of her mind where her pastry was concerned. "I'll do that."

She hung up, emotionally and physically exhausted. She couldn't deal with anything more that night. Maybe a solution would come to her in the morning.

Zoe climbed the stairs, her feet like dead weights at the bottom of her legs. Once inside her bedroom, she paused long enough to lock the door and remove her jeans. Then she burrowed beneath the soft blankets she'd piled on the floor and prayed for the blessed release sleep would bring.

5

The sound of a loud bang followed closely by a cacophony of male voices brought Zoe instantly awake. Memories of the previous night flooded in, weighing her down. She groaned as she turned over to reach for her phone, her muscles stiff from sleeping on the hard floor.

She blinked a few times in the early morning light, trying to clear her vision so she could read the clock.

Seven a.m.? Who the hell made so much noise that early in the morning?

Asher.

She rolled to her knees and slowly stood. Her arms and legs ached from all the packing, cleaning, and moving she'd done the previous day. At least tonight, she'd be able to sleep in her own bed even if she didn't know if it was in her own house.

Trying to stay steady on her feet, she slipped on a pair of yoga pants, pushed her tangled hair out of her face, and unlocked the bedroom door.

She jerked to a stop. One more step, and she would have collided with the mattress whizzing past her room.

"Morning," Asher said as he passed, carrying the tail end of the mattress.

Zoe rolled her eyes and shook her head, allowing her gaze to follow him down the hall to his room. His triceps bulged from the weight of his load, and his tight gray tee outlined the muscles in his broad shoulders and back. When she realized she was gawking, she palmed the side of her head, hoping to knock sense into herself.

She couldn't deny he looked good. But she also knew firsthand his allure went no further than his looks. And that she could do without.

She made her way across the hall into the bathroom and firmly closed the door behind her. Fifteen minutes later, she came out refreshed and rejuvenated as much as she could without her coffee.

"Hey, Zoe," Kade said as he passed her, carrying two stacked boxes.

Noelle's fiancée was more or less a newcomer to their town. He'd grown up in Pinecone Valley, a good twenty minutes away, but had migrated to their town to open a new motel next to Rumors. Reluctantly, Noelle had fallen for his dark hair, brown eyes, and sexy half smile. Zoe couldn't say she blamed her.

"Hey, wait a minute," she called after him. "I thought you were helping *me* move."

Kade disappeared into Asher's room without a reply, but returned a few seconds later.

"I am," he said and wiped his brow. "But you weren't awake when I arrived with your stuff, so I thought I'd help out my buddy, Asher. He told me what Old Man Jenkins did, and that you're both going to stay here until the situation is resolved. I think that's great that you two can work together."

Zoe held up a hand. "Please do not start singing the praises of Asher Campbell to me. I don't want to lose my appetite before I can sink my teeth into one of Noelle's cinnamon rolls."

Kade chuckled. "Asher's a good guy."

She shook her head in mock disappointment. "What did I just say?"

"Okay, fine. Noelle did warn me. But, hey, maybe you'll get to see a different side of him during the next couple of days. Or weeks. Or months. Who knows how long it will take to track down that rogue Jenkins?" He grinned, and she knew he teased her, but still.

"God forbid it will be longer than a couple of days." She put a hand on her hip. "You do realize that when the verdict comes back, one of us will probably ask for help again. You could be doing all this for nothing."

He sobered. "Yeah, I thought of that. I'm really sorry this happened to both of you. Jenkins has some answering to do."

"If they can find him." Her attempts to remain lighthearted fizzled. "I received a message from Milo this morning. No one seems to know where to look."

Kade lifted one side of his mouth in a commiserating smile. "I know it's hard, but have faith it'll work out for the best. Asher said you're both taking your documents to the sheriff's office today. Are you riding together?"

Sounds of someone struggling to get through the front door rose to meet them. She eyed Kade. "Umm...no. It's bad enough being trapped in a house. I can't escape him in a car."

He grinned and shook his head. "All right. I won't mention it." He shifted his gaze to the bottom of the stairs. "Let me help you with that, man."

Kade hustled down and grabbed the opposite end of a chest of drawers. "How'd you get that this far?"

"Muscles," Asher said as they headed up the stairs. He gave

her a look as he passed that said he was plenty proud of his abilities. "We're doing your stuff next."

"Great," she called after him. She didn't want him anywhere near her things, but she couldn't begrudge Kade the extra help. "Just put the bed in the bedroom, the kitchen table in the kitchen, and everything else wherever you want. I'll be back in a while to take care of the rest."

"Are you headed into Pinecone?" Asher asked as he returned to the hall, catching her before she reached the bottom of the stairs.

She wasn't about to account for her comings and goings. They weren't roommates. Just two strangers sharing a common space for a short, hopefully tolerable period. "Among other things."

"Do you mind taking my paperwork with you? I made copies last night."

She lifted her brows, letting him know his request annoyed her.

He gave her a smile that was sexier than it should have been for a dirty, sweaty guy. "Come on. You're headed there anyway, and I'll be doing you a favor by moving your stuff. Seems like a fair trade."

Yes, unfortunately, it did. Damn. She needed to rein herself in before she became a person she didn't want to be. "Fine. I'd be happy to."

"Thanks." He lifted the bottom of his shirt to wipe his brow and flashed an amazing set of abs that she wished she could unsee. She blinked and looked away. At that moment, she didn't know who was worse. Him for his shabby treatment of her in the past, or her for being remotely attracted to him despite it.

He thumbed toward the kitchen. "I think I left them on the counter. Would you mind grabbing them?"

She gave him a chilled smile. "Not at all."

———

Zoe sagged in her chair at Rumors. "I can't do it, Noelle. I can't live there with him for days or worse, weeks until someone locates Jenkins."

Noelle reached out and patted her arm. "But you already said you're afraid if you leave, you'll lose the place."

She squeezed her eyes shut as desperation rolled through her. "I know," she ground out between clenched teeth.

Noelle called out her goodbye to a customer, and then she leaned forward, her elbows on the small café table. "So here's my best advice. *Suck it up.*"

Zoe snorted and leaned back. "Easier said than done."

"He's kind of cute," Noelle offered.

"Only on the outside." She released a deep breath and soothed her emotions with a large bite of cinnamon roll. "It's going to be torture," she said around a mouthful.

"Don't be dramatic." Noelle never had a problem calling her on her behavior.

She pouted. "But it's just so unfair. This was my house, my life, and now Asher's jumped right in the middle of it. What if a judge or someone else decides Asher owns it, and I paid for a house that Jenkins no longer had the right to sell? I'm guessing whoever bought it first is the owner, but I'm too scared to ask Asher when he did. I don't want to give him any motivation to kick me out."

"I don't know what to tell you. Unless..." Noelle cleared her throat, putting on a serious face. "I can't believe I'm going to suggest this."

Zoe leaned forward. "Tell me. I'm desperate. I'll do anything."

"You have to promise first," Noelle said in a lowered voice so other customers couldn't hear. "You can tell no one that I was the mastermind behind this plan, understand?"

"I swear." If Noelle was making her promise, then it had to be good. "Tell me already."

"What if Asher decided to leave? What if you *helped* him to decide to leave?"

"You mean force him out?" Zoe narrowed her gaze, trying to understand her friend's suggestion.

"Not force. *Encourage.* Make him see that it's in his best interest." She shrugged, giving Zoe a hopeful look.

Zoe slowly nodded as ideas filtered through her mind. "Find something that really drives him crazy and do that over and over."

"Exactly."

"Something like…a baby. Especially one that cries. He admitted he couldn't stay at Milo and Anna's any longer because their little one cries too much. It must be annoying the hell out of him."

Noelle's eyes sparkled with mischief. "It's worth a shot, I think. But again, you can't tell anyone. Asher's a good friend of Seth and April, and I know it would make April really sad to hear of our plot. I'm only suggesting it because you need someone to bolster you."

Emotion tugged at her. "Thank you for that." She'd had so few people on her side throughout her life, and she knew the value of a good friend.

"So, babies. Who do we know?"

Zoe gasped as an idea struck. "Who better than Anna? I'm going to call and offer my babysitting services right away."

———

When Zoe arrived home that afternoon, she was shocked to see how much furniture Asher had moved into her house. He'd put a nice leather couch where she'd intended to put her chair. A big screen TV. Lamps. Hell, even a potted plant. If nothing else, he'd made it clear he intended to stay.

"Looks like you're all settled in," she said, trying to keep the sarcasm from her voice.

He looked up from the game he watched on TV and shrugged. "I'd rather have my stuff here than in a friend's barn where it might get damaged."

She supposed she could understand that. She'd probably want the same if her stuff was as nice as his. "Looks like Dana didn't get everything in the divorce."

His pleasant expression turned to a frown.

Now, who was being the jerk? "Sorry. I didn't mean it like that."

"Forget it," he said and turned toward the TV. "She got the house, but she sure as hell wasn't entitled to everything inside."

Zoe had heard the rumors, how Dana had booted him out, and then moved her new boyfriend in before the sheets had cooled. "You didn't take the bed, did you?"

He shot her an irritated gaze. "No."

"Good," she said, folding her arms in front of her. She hadn't meant to goad him and bring up bad memories, but if she had a significant other and he'd cheated on her, she'd burn the damn bed, mattress and all.

He ignored her and stayed focused on his game.

"One more thing." She pulled the Rumors paper bag from her purse. "I'm putting this cinnamon roll in the kitchen. If you touch it, I will hunt you down."

He glanced at her then, his expression softening. "Sorry about that. I thought it was a housewarming gift."

"It was. From me *to* me." She held up a hand when he started to speak. "Never mind. I'm going upstairs."

It was pointless to have these conversations. She didn't like him, and he'd obviously never liked her. Her best option was to avoid him completely, if possible.

6

Rain fell from the darkened sky as Zoe drove from her accounting job at City Hall to the little house on the outskirts of town. She'd imagined many times what it would have been like to arrive at home at the end of a long day and find happiness in her very own sanctuary. After a quiet dinner, she could garden, read on the porch, or take a walk down to the river at night and listen to the crickets.

The sight of Asher's truck sitting in the drive was a streak of black slashed across her lovely watercolor picture. It was the first time all week that he'd beaten her home, and now she wouldn't get that blessed hour of peace where she could make her dinner and head to her room before he arrived.

Living with him was quite the opposite of what she'd pictured her life to be like. She'd been thrust into an untenable position with a man she couldn't tolerate indefinitely. It was literally hell.

She parked her car and struggled to straighten her thoughts. They'd managed civility for the past few days. No reason to expect otherwise today.

When she entered the house, the smell of something delicious beckoned, and her stomach cheered in response. She dropped her purse and jacket on the couch and cautiously made her way into the kitchen. Asher stood over the stove stirring whatever he'd made in a big pot. He seemed lost in his thoughts and looked completely at home in his blue t-shirt, flannel pants, and bare feet.

"You're home early," she said.

His gaze jumped to her as though she'd startled him, and the look he gave her sent an awkward tendril of desire twisting through her. "We got rained out."

"Oh. That's too bad." For him and for her.

She walked to the fridge, acting as normal as she could, wishing she wasn't so hyperaware of him all the time. She opened the door and reviewed the contents. She'd make a quick salad, she decided, and be out of his way in a short amount of time.

"I made dinner," he said.

She turned to him and hesitated, not sure what to say.

He watched her with cautious eyes. "Chicken noodle soup sounded good on a rainy day," he offered.

She wasn't used to this somber side of him, and he seemed somehow vulnerable, which tugged at her heart. "Oh, okay. Thank you. It smells really good."

Asher lifted his chin. "You want to grab some bowls? It's ready to eat."

With thoughts whirling inside her head, she pulled dishes from the cupboard. She wanted to trust that he could be civil, but it seemed like a mistake. Still, if things turned awful, she could always walk out.

And the soup did sound perfect.

She headed in his direction as a thick bolt of lightning cracked the sky beyond the large picture window. A powerful boom of thunder quickly followed, making her flinch. "Whoa. That's really close."

Rain poured down in sheets, scouring the earth and everything on it. Beautiful to watch, but she was glad she was inside.

He shifted his gaze from the window to her. "I think it's supposed to rain off and on all night. Meteorologist said there's a row of storms lined up."

She held out the bowls, and he ladled soup into each of them. "I guess it's good. We need the rain."

"Yeah," he said, but his less than enthusiastic tone showed he didn't agree. "It will cut into my paycheck, though. If I don't work, I don't get paid."

"I guess that's true." She placed the bowls on the table, turned to go back for drinks, and collided with Asher. He caught her in his embrace.

"Oh, sorry," she said. "I didn't realize you were right behind me."

He stared down at her for a moment, stirring her interest. "No harm."

She had never been so close to him. At this distance, she could see each individual eyelash that framed his misty gray eyes. His fingers singed her skin where he held her, and her body's reaction to him stunned her.

She gave a soft laugh to diffuse the suddenly electric situation, but it did little good.

He stepped back and released her from his grasp, seeming affected by their unexpected interaction as well.

She circled around him, as though nothing had happened beyond an accidental bump, and headed for the fridge. "Can I get you something to drink? I have milk or water or there are a couple of beers in the back."

"Milk, thanks."

She filled two glasses and returned, taking a seat across

from him at the small wooden table she'd found at a garage sale. She briefly glanced at him, afraid to meet his gaze, but he seemed lost in his thoughts once again.

He'd already started eating his soup, and she was at a loss for what to say to him. Instead of speaking, she picked up her spoon and tasted the soup.

Delicious flavors burst across her tongue, stealing attention away from other thoughts. She nearly groaned from pleasure. "Oh, wow. This is really good."

He lifted his gaze as a small but genuine smile crossed his lips. "Glad you like it."

"Like it? I love it. Don't tell Noelle or April, but this is better than theirs."

He chuckled at that. "Nah."

Since they'd started talking, she felt compelled to keep the lighthearted conversation going. "Where did you learn to cook?"

He snorted. "My ex."

"Ah," she said as awkwardness filled the space between them like weeds in a fertile garden. Maybe thoughts of Dana were what had caused his distracted state. "At least one good thing came from your time together."

He scoffed in disgust. "There is that. All I know is if you dabble with love, you'd better be prepared to get burned."

She didn't exactly like the guy, but she wasn't completely heartless. "Are you okay, Asher?"

He huffed a breath. "Yeah, I'm fine. I'll be fine. Just weighing my options if this house thing doesn't work out."

She exhaled as his worries echoed hers. "Have you heard anything from the sheriff's office?"

"No. I called today, but they haven't found any leads yet. It's like Jenkins disappeared off the face of the earth."

The stress of worrying and wondering had eaten at her for

days, but she hadn't considered that Asher might be feeling the same. "Maybe we shouldn't talk about this right now. Maybe we should enjoy our soup instead."

The sound of the doorbell ringing saved him from responding. "I'll get it," he said and stood.

She glanced at the clock, remembered her plans for the evening, and hurried to shove the last bites of soup into her mouth before she stood as well. That would be Anna showing up with Baby Kiley.

She carried her dishes to the sink and then rushed into the living room to find Milo and Anna standing inside the front door, water droplets shimmering on their clothes. The couple had dressed up for the evening, Milo looking handsome in a white button-down shirt tucked into black jeans. Anna wore a lovely red sundress that highlighted her dark hair, while Kiley slept soundly in her arms.

"Thanks so much for doing this for us, Zoe." Anna held out the diaper bag to her, and she placed it on the couch.

"Yeah, we sure appreciate it," Milo added. "We haven't had much in the way of proper dates since this little darlin' came along."

Anna smiled lovingly at her husband, stirring twinges of jealousy inside Zoe.

"She'll be hungry when she wakes up," Anna said. "There's a bottle in the bag. We should be back in two hours."

Zoe flicked a glance at Asher and found him staring at her with raised brows. She flashed him an innocent smile as Anna slid her baby into Zoe's arms. The sweet bundle made soft noises and then settled back to sleep. "Take your time. Kiley will be fine here."

A yearning to have her own child someday welled inside Zoe. "She's adorable. We're going to have a great time."

"You two doing okay?" Milo looked from Zoe to Asher. "Looks like you both decided to stay."

Zoe slid a sideways glance at Asher. "Doing okay."

Milo's words were a stark reminder that she and Asher were playing for different teams, and she was determined that Team Cassidy would triumph. She hoped the cops found Jenkins before he spent all of Asher's money, because he would need it when he moved out.

"Great. Just great," Asher said before heading toward the kitchen.

Anna lifted her brows, and Zoe shrugged.

"Don't worry about us," Zoe said. "Go have a good time. We'll be fine."

The Sykes closed the door on the way out as more thunder shook the house. Zoe stood still, staring at the precious baby in her arms, suddenly in awe of her new responsibilities. Offering to watch the one child who'd driven Asher from the last place he'd lived had seemed like the best idea. But she hadn't exactly considered what would be required on her part.

Still, two or three hours. She could manage that. Little Kiley was sound asleep and might stay that way for much of the time. Holding the sweet child and listening to the rain pounding on the roof sounded like an ideal evening. And when she woke, Zoe would give her a bottle, check her diaper, change it if necessary, and they could hang out the rest of the time. No problem.

She couldn't understand why Asher had such an issue with Kiley. She was so adorably cute. Maybe he was one of those guys who didn't like babies.

If so, that would work for her benefit, too.

7

Kiley blessed Zoe with ten minutes of peaceful sleeping before she opened her eyes. Slowly, she focused on Zoe's face.

"Hi there," Zoe cooed.

The baby stared for a moment, then scrunched her features and released all the air in her lungs in a shrill wail. The sound ripped through Zoe like the grim reaper's scythe, and she jumped up from the couch with the screaming baby in her arms.

"Oh no. I'm sorry. Shh... I know I'm not your mommy, but this will be okay. *Shit.* I mean not shit because babies don't need to hear that word. I mean...hell, let's get your bottle."

Kiley continued to screech, her tiny arms shaking as she flailed them about. Zoe leaned her against her shoulder and patted her back before snatching the diaper bag and making her way into the kitchen. The patting seemed to calm her, but only for a few seconds. Then her howls started again. She was shocked such a loud sound could come from a tiny baby.

Asher looked up from whatever he'd been doing on his

phone as she entered. He shook his head slightly as though to say I told you so and pushed away from the table.

"It's fine. We're fine. I'm actually thinking I might do this regularly to earn some extra income," she said over Kiley's cries. Hopefully that would be enough to make him want to leave, because she wasn't sure she could keep her composure for much longer.

His stare contained zero emotion. "Is that so?"

She couldn't tell if he was annoyed or not. But right now, that didn't matter. She needed to soothe Kiley.

She juggled the diaper bag and crying baby as she set the bag on the counter and tried to unzip it. Her fingers fumbled, so she pinned the bag between her and the counter to hold it steady while she tried again. If Kiley would stop crying for a minute, she could manage her task much better.

Suddenly, the bag slid from her grasp, and she whirled to find Asher just beyond her elbow with the diaper bag in hand. He slid the zipper open and removed the bottle. Without saying a word, he moved to the sink and turned on the hot water. Then he pulled a bowl from the cupboard and stood while the water poured into it.

Zoe bounced the baby and feverishly patted her back while she watched him work. "What are you doing?"

He slid a sideways look at her and lifted a brow. "You have to warm the bottle, Zoe."

"Oh. Anna didn't mention that." How was she supposed to know? She'd never held a baby before, let alone care for one.

"It's common knowledge."

She ached to wipe the smug look off his face. If she didn't have her hands full, she would have. Once again, he had to belittle her and make her feel stupid. She turned away from him, refusing to let him see how easily his words could cut her.

"Shh..." she whispered into Kiley's ear. The tiny tot calmed slightly, so Zoe repeated her actions. "It's going to be okay." She wished someone would tell her the same thing.

"Here you go," Asher said, coming up behind her.

She met his gaze, trying to keep hers as neutral as possible.

"Hold out your wrist," he demanded.

She complied. "Why?" she asked over the baby's crying.

He tipped the bottle upside down and sprinkled a few drops of the bottle's contents onto her arm. "Warm, but not hot?"

She nodded.

"Then you're good to go." He held out the bottle. "Make sure you keep the bottom upright so she doesn't swallow air."

Zoe couldn't bring herself to thank him, although she was eternally grateful. Instead, she took the bottle and headed for the living room, where she could breathe. She resumed her seat and positioned Kiley in her arms like she'd seen on TV. She tipped the bottle toward her mouth and the greedy infant suckled like she was a starved baby.

"Lordy," she whispered, grateful for the reprieve. "You babies are a fussy lot."

Kiley drank a good portion of her dinner before she squirmed. Zoe lifted the bottle and examined the contents. "You didn't drink it all."

Were they supposed to? It was probably a good thing she wasn't a mother. No infant would survive her.

The tiny baby curled inward and then flung her arms and legs outward again as another cry pierced the quiet like a needle through her thumb.

"Oh, no." Zoe cradled her and bounced her, but Kiley wouldn't relent. She tried the bottle again, but Kiley refused it. "What honey? Tell me what I'm doing wrong." If she couldn't calm her, she'd likely lose her mind before Anna ever returned.

"Did you burp her?" Asher asked as he stood in the doorway between kitchen and living room.

She startled, making Kiley cry harder. "How do I do that?" she asked, the tone of her voice echoing her frustration. By the look on his face, she was sure he was about to snicker.

"Don't laugh," she said between gritted teeth.

"I'm not." But he sure as hell looked like he might. "Hold her over your shoulder and gently but firmly pat her back."

With exasperation nipping at her like vicious hounds at her heels, she did as he suggested, keeping her gaze away from his. Repeatedly, she patted as hard as she dared, which wasn't very hard. Kiley kept on crying, and Zoe finally looked to Asher for reassurance. "Am I doing this right?"

He nodded. "You are. Keep patting. It'll come."

She wanted to break down and sob like the baby. *It's common knowledge* kept repeating in her head. She wanted to call him on it, ask him why he was always such a jerk to her, but she had all she could handle at the moment.

A loud belch that surely didn't come from that tiny baby vibrated through the air like a sonic blast. As Zoe pulled Kiley away from her shoulder, a slew of formula came rushing out of her mouth and slopped all over Zoe's blouse. Kiley's eyes grew wide, and she looked as surprised as Zoe that she'd puked.

"Ah, shit," Asher said and hurried to the kitchen. He returned with a bundle of paper towels and began wiping Kiley's clothes. "Here, let me take her. You'll probably want to change."

Zoe stared at one face and then the other, not knowing what to say. Between the two of them, they'd broken her. She had nothing left. She turned and headed up the stairs, her emotions frozen as she found an old t-shirt and a clean bra.

With mechanical steps, she entered the bathroom and closed the door. She plugged the sink's drain, turned on the water, and removed her blouse. Gobs of disgusting white stuff covered her shirt. Some had even gone over her shoulder.

She soaked the blouse while she wiped off and donned fresh clothes. Was she forever doomed to be that girl? The one with a crazy mom, the one who struggled to fit in with everyone else, the one who obviously had no clue what to do with a baby and so many other things. Would she be ridiculed forever?

She hated everything so much at the moment. The damned house. The crying baby. Asher. Most of all, Asher.

It took her a few minutes to gather herself. She wrung out her blouse and hung it over the shower rod and then washed her hands and face. When she'd regained control, she unlocked the bathroom door and stepped into the hall.

She probably shouldn't have deserted Asher with the baby for as long as she had, but she couldn't hear any bawling, so maybe they were okay.

Surprisingly, they weren't in the living room when she arrived downstairs. She checked the kitchen, and they weren't there either.

He wouldn't have left, so...

She peeked out the front window to make sure his truck was still in the drive and caught sight of him sitting on the front porch swing with little Kiley cuddled against his chest. He'd wrapped a blanket around her tiny body and softly patted her while they swung.

Zoe quietly stepped outside into the rain-soaked, muggy air. Lightning lit the distant sky, but the worst of the storm had passed. She dropped her jaw when she realized the baby was fast asleep and Asher had his lids half closed. Why was it so easy for him?

He gave her a small smile and patted the seat next to him as he slowed the rocking motion.

"How did you do that?" She kept her voice lowered so she wouldn't wake Kiley as she sat.

"Magic touch. All the babies love me." He resumed swinging.

She gave a soft snort. "If you're a magical baby-whisperer, why can't you handle staying at Milo's?"

He lifted his brows in mock disgust. "You've heard her. Day in and day out, it wears on you. Honestly, you're a saint for volunteering to watch her so Milo and Anna could have a break. I'm sure they needed it."

She swallowed a lump of guilt for the true reason behind Kiley's presence. "I guess I didn't realize what I'd gotten myself into."

He chuckled. "She's certainly a handful. I hope my kids, when I have some, aren't as difficult."

She slid a glance in his direction, noticing the way his strong hand rested on Kiley's tiny back and realized, despite his assholery toward her, he would make a good dad. "You want kids?"

"Sure. A couple." His deep voice resonated through the warm summer air. "You?"

"I don't know. Maybe. I haven't given it much thought." She had a hard enough time managing herself most days. "Not if they're this tough."

He released a soft chuckle. "They're not so bad. You just have to figure them out first, and they're all different."

"How is it you're so knowledgeable about baby things?"

"Time with this one. Plus, my sister has kids." His chin wrinkled as he tilted his head against his chest to look at Kiley. "But seriously, how could you not want something so sweet?"

Dangerously powerful desire tugged on her heart and left her wondering. "Yeah, I could handle it as long as I'd have you around to whisper in her ear and keep her human."

She half-choked when she realized what she'd said. "I didn't mean it like that. Not that you'd have to be around. Just a baby-whisperer. Any baby-whisperer." Ah, God. She should stop.

A grin curved his lips, and she forced herself to look away. She didn't want to like him, didn't want to see him as anything other than a jerk. Then she wouldn't feel as bad when she took his house, or she'd feel justified in hating him if he took hers. This...this was not okay.

She needed to remember the humiliation he'd caused her. None of his current behavior made up for that. She checked her watch and then folded her arms across her chest. "Looks like we only have one more hour to go."

Thank God it wasn't longer.

8

Asher and Seth each lifted large sheets of plywood and carried them into the half-finished house they were building. Asher carefully walked across the wood joists and laid the next sheet of plywood into place.

Seth placed the board he held against a four-by-four. "How is it, living with the one woman who truly hates your guts? Must be a pleasant way to spend your days."

Asher pulled a screw from his pouch and drilled it in place. "It's not too bad, actually. I think I'm growing on her, especially after I saved her last night."

Concern wrinkled Seth's brow. "Yeah? What did you do?"

"For some unknown, godforsaken reason, she'd offered to watch Kiley for Milo and Anna." He shook his head in disbelief. "You and I both know that kid's a handful, and Zoe doesn't know the first thing about babies. So I helped her out. Showed off my baby-whispering skills." He liked the nickname Zoe had given him.

Seth snorted. "Baby whisperer?"

"Hey, I have other talents besides construction," he called

over his shoulder as he finished securing the plywood into place.

His friend scoffed. "Babysitting one night doesn't make you an expert. Wait until you have one full time."

Asher stood and caught his friend's smile. "I thought you enjoyed being a dad."

"I do. Greatest thing that's ever happened to me. Doesn't mean it's easy."

Asher had always believed he and Dana would have had children. When he was first married, it had been easy to see himself as a dad to a couple of kids. Now, he couldn't picture getting married again, let alone becoming a father, even though he'd told Zoe he wanted to.

Seth heaved a weighted sigh and shook his head.

His friend's sudden shift in behavior caught him off guard. "What?"

Seth hesitated for a moment before speaking. "I know you've had a crush on Zoe for years. Probably still do, so this question might piss you off."

An uncomfortable twinge crept across him like a nasty spider. "Spit it out."

Seth pinned him with a sharp look. "Do you find it strange Zoe would offer to babysit the one child you're trying to avoid?"

"No. Not really." Not until Seth mentioned it. "You think this is a ploy? To irritate me? To get me to move out?" He didn't want to believe Zoe would be that devious, but he discovered once before he couldn't trust a woman. "She doesn't seem like a conniving person to me."

"Maybe she's desperate," Seth tossed back to him. "After all, she hates your guts."

"She doesn't hate my guts." He wasn't sure why, but she'd warmed to him slightly. "Things are okay between us."

Maybe even good for a few moments the previous evening.

His peace offering of soup had brought a smile to her face, and he'd enjoyed their quiet meal together with the raging storm as a backdrop. Had he known her better, he would have called it romantic.

Seth blew out a long breath. "That's good."

When Asher tried to head out for more plywood, Seth put a hand on his shoulder, stopping him from leaving the room. "There's more. I didn't want to say anything. Didn't want to stir the pot if it wasn't true, but now I'm wondering."

Asher shrugged off his touch. The uncomfortable look on his friend's face told him it wouldn't be good news. "I already know Dana wants to get married again."

"Yeah, I know, but it's not that."

He didn't know what could hurt him worse than Dana's demoralizing news. "What then?"

Seth cocked his head, studying him. "I think you nailed it with what you just guessed. Earlene Smith caught me outside Rumors the other day and mentioned she'd heard Zoe planning to babysit as a way to get you to leave. Since you don't like kids and all. Earlene thought someone should tell you."

All Asher could do was shake his head as deep disappointment rolled through him.

Seth shrugged. "Take it for what it is. We all know what a busybody that woman can be. I only mentioned it because Zoe did babysit last night. Don't believe it if you don't want to, but be careful where she's concerned."

"Yeah." Goddammit. Just when he'd believed things were going well. "She did tell me the other night when Kiley was screaming that she was considering babysitting regularly to earn extra money."

"Yet she has little experience in that area." Seth shook his head. "That seems underhanded to me."

World-weary pain pierced his shield. He'd done it again.

He'd thought he might have a shot with Zoe this time around. But after all these years, he needed to get a clue. She wasn't interested in him. Never would be.

"You're the one who reminded me how much she hates me," Asher said. "It shouldn't be all that surprising that she'd try a stunt like this. It backfired on her, though. She was the one who was a wreck by the time Anna and Milo returned. Me? I've been living with that baby's cries for weeks, so I have a few tricks up my sleeve." He could at least laugh about that.

His friend chuckled. "Serves her right then."

"I actually felt sorry for her last night." Asher scratched the scruff on his chin, trying to push off his disillusionment, but anger replaced it. He never thought he'd be one to become so distrustful of women, but the naysayers might know what they're talking about after all. "I thought we'd come to an amicable agreement, but apparently, I'm the only one playing fair."

Seth gave him a sympathetic nod. "Whatcha gonna do about it?"

He wasn't going to take it lying down, that was for damn sure. "Fire a counter shot. Do something that will drive *her* crazy. Like invite my rowdiest buddies to come over and watch a few games, drink some beer. Stay up late when she has to work early the next morning."

"You'll be getting up early for work, too," Seth reminded him.

"Doesn't matter. Not if I can get her the hell out of *my* house. The sooner, the better." If she wanted to play dirty, he'd give her more mud than she could handle.

———

Early evening had set in by the time Zoe found her way back to the kitchen table, prepared to calculate the quarterly estimated taxes for a small business that had hired her on the side. A cooler front with more rain had rolled through earlier in the day, and she'd opened all the windows to catch the fresh breeze.

If she could have had her home the way she wanted it, the way it should be, her home office would be set up by now. Unfortunately, there was a man's bed occupying that room.

Still, it was a lovely evening, and she relished the solitude whenever she could get it.

The sound of truck tires crunching on the gravel drive pulled her from her work. She glanced at the clock, surprised to find it so late. Asher had been arriving home much earlier in the evening, limited by what they could do in the bad weather. But not tonight, and she wondered what might have kept him this time.

She waited a few moments, expecting him to walk into the kitchen to find his dinner. Instead, he fired up the TV. She mentally shrugged and returned to tallying numbers.

The sound of a male voice other than Asher's was next to steal her attention, and she turned, trying to decipher who it belonged to.

"Be right back," Asher said in response to his friend.

A few seconds later, he popped into the kitchen. "Oh, hey," he said, as though surprised to find her there. He held up a twelve-pack of Bud. "I'm just going to put this in the fridge."

She arched a brow. "Is someone else here?"

"A buddy of mine." He shut the fridge door and then leaned against the counter to remove a dirty work boot. He let it drop haphazardly to the floor with a thud and then proceeded to do the same with the other.

She frowned but said nothing.

He pulled his dusty shirt over his head with one hand and left it bunched on the counter next to her bowl of apples. "We're gonna watch a game."

She blinked, trying not to look at his muscled chest, and focused instead on the ire building inside her. "Just don't get too loud, okay? I'm trying to work."

He shrugged as he poured cinnamon bears into a bowl and then grabbed a bag of chips. "Sure. No problem."

With that, he disappeared into the other room, and she did her best to ignore his discarded clothing and boots while she reviewed the numbers in front of her, trying to remember where she'd left off.

A few minutes later, the doorbell rang, and she groaned in disgust. *Really?*

More male voices joined the fray and, before long, the heavenly scent of pizza wafted in to tempt her. It had been a couple of hours since she'd had her salad, and the thought of all those delicious carbs and gooey cheese made her stomach rumble in protest.

She looked up as Jeremy Duncan walked into the room. He definitely had it going in the looks department with his short, dark hair and dark brown eyes, but not so much where brains were concerned.

"Zoe," he said in greeting. "I'd heard you and Asher were shacking up while the cops look for Jenkins."

She managed a smile. "I wouldn't call it shacking up, Jeremy. More like co-habitating."

He frowned and then nodded. "Yeah, whatever I guess." He dismissed her in favor of a couple of beers from the fridge.

She'd barely begun working again when the doorbell rang for the second time. She threw her pen in the air in a dramatic show of frustration. "This is ridiculous," she mumbled.

"Hey," Asher said as he returned to the kitchen and opened

the fridge. He now wore a fresh shirt and flannel pants. She wanted to ask why he couldn't have discarded all his clothing in his bedroom when he'd changed, but she stayed silent.

"We're not bothering you, are we?"

Inflammatory words hovered on her tongue, but she wouldn't give him the satisfaction. "Maybe a little."

"I'll tell the guys to keep it down." He smiled and gave her a nod before he left once again.

Her stomach growled, begging her to ignore work and go play. A hefty cheer echoed from the adjacent room like a call to action. "Sweet purgatory." She dropped her head into her hands. It would be impossible to focus on her work with them in the other room.

She closed out the computer program and logged off her laptop. She'd finish this tomorrow when the house was quiet once again. For now, she'd soak in her lovely tub and let the guys hoot and holler all they wanted.

Asher looked up when she emerged from the kitchen. "You should watch with us, Zo."

The friendly use of her nickname irritated her further. "No, thanks."

She glanced at his friends, recognizing Seth Collier in addition to Jeremy. But a new guy she hadn't met with longer blond hair and biceps the size of a small dog looked like he could cause some serious trouble if he wanted.

Resigned, she headed toward the stairs. When she reached the first step, she glanced back and caught Asher sharing a look of satisfaction with Seth. The exchange caught her off guard and caused her to misstep. She gripped the railing as thoughts tumbled in her head.

Was this payback for their night with Kiley? Did he have a plan similar to hers?

She stewed as she climbed each stair. By the time she

turned on the tub's faucet, she'd convinced herself Asher had his own agenda to run her off. If she'd thought of it, why wouldn't he?

"Rotten dog," she whispered as she slipped into the water. If he thought his friends would send her packing, he had another thing coming. She'd grown up around plenty of less-than-stellar people. Those guys were nothing in comparison.

The warm water and lavender scented bubble bath did little to ease her annoyance, but soaking in the tub gave her plenty of time to consider her options. When all was said and done, the phrase, "if you can't beat 'em, join 'em" sounded like a damn good idea. She wasn't above watching a good game of hockey. In fact, sometimes she enjoyed it.

One thing was for sure. She'd relish watching Asher's reaction when she had more fun with his friends than he did.

She climbed from the tub, wrapped a fluffy towel around her, and hastened to her bedroom. There, she tossed on a t-shirt and a pair of flannel shorts, figuring she'd follow his casual lead. At the very least, she knew she could command Jeremy's attention. That alone might be enough to put a burr under Asher's butt.

Asher raised his brows as she descended the stairs, and she sent him a sweet smile in return, as though he and his buddies hadn't affected her in the least. In the kitchen, she helped herself to a beer from the fridge. Her house, her fridge, made it fair game. She popped the top as she glared at his smelly shirt sitting on the counter. *Gross.*

"Yeah," several of the guys yelled as she returned, their gazes glued to the TV. Asher punched the air in his excitement and then lost all enthusiasm when she stepped between the two chairs and headed for the couch.

"Is there room for me?" she asked Jeremy and the newcomer.

"Sure," Jeremy answered with a grin.

"Hell, yeah," said the stranger, and patted the cushion between him and Jeremy. The man gave her a friendly smile, his blond mustache and goatee highlighting sensual lips.

Satisfaction washed over her like a hot summer's rain as his friends played right into her plans. Dear Asher was about to find out exactly what kind of opponent he'd come up against.

9

Zoe settled between Jeremy and the hot-looking bad boy before she slid a subtle glance Asher's way. He stared with a none-too-happy look on his face. She shrugged. "I hope you don't care that I changed my mind. You guys sounded like you're having so much fun."

With a blink, she switched her gaze to the TV and worked to keep the smug smile from emerging on her face.

The guy next to her nudged her with his elbow. "I'm Roger. You're Zo?"

"Zoe," she corrected. "But you can call me Zo."

He grinned as mischief sparkled in his startling blue eyes. "I'll call you Zoe, if that's okay with you." He had dangerous distraction written all over him. Normally, she'd steer clear of a guy like that, but these were special circumstances.

"Of course." She smiled and leaned into the couch cushion as she took a drink of beer. If nothing else, she'd enjoy Roger's company.

The next time their team scored, Roger scooted to the edge of his seat with a holler. *"Hell, yeah. We're killing 'em."*

"Damn straight," Jeremy said.

Their enthusiasm infected her, and she added her own words of excitement. Roger shifted a sideways glance in her direction and gave her an irresistible smile. When he finally sat back, he was several inches closer. Close enough that their elbows touched.

"You and Asher an item?" he asked in a low voice.

She shook her head. "Unfortunate roommates for a short period of time. It's a long story."

He gave her an understanding nod and then shifted his gaze to the TV. A second later, he glanced at her again, a mischievous smile on his face. "I'm single, in case you're wondering."

She snorted, surprised by his candor. "Okay," she said with a laugh.

"Just thought I'd put it out there." He grinned again and took a drink of his beer.

Zoe focused on the game. This really was more fun than she'd expected. Everyone seemed to be getting into the game, except Asher. His emotions had taken a downward turn. More than once, she caught him frowning at her and Roger. She wanted to ask him what his problem was, but she had a good idea. His fault, though. He was the one who'd brought it on.

At the end of the second period, she stood. "Anyone need another beer?"

"I'll take one," Jeremy said.

"Not me." Seth unfolded himself from his chair. "I need to head out. Told April I'd be home by nine."

"Seriously, dude?" Roger said. "You let a woman tell you what to do?"

Seth could have taken offense, she certainly had, but he only shrugged and smiled. "What can I say? What she's got going on at home beats what you all got here." He tipped his head toward Asher. "See you tomorrow."

She directed her question to Roger. "What's wrong with a woman calling the shots sometimes?"

"Why would you want to, darlin'?" He held up a hand before she could respond. "Don't be getting mad at me now. Just men and women are better at different things."

Meaning he believed men should always be in control? She thought about setting him straight, but he wasn't worth the energy it would take. Instead, she took herself to the kitchen and retrieved beers for her and Jeremy. Because she'd offered, and it was a nice thing to do. Not because she was a woman who waited on men.

When she returned, she took Seth's empty seat instead of returning to the couch.

"What's wrong, darlin'?" Roger asked. "I don't smell, do I?"

Either her beer had gotten the best of her, or this whole evening had suddenly gone south. She sent him a friendly enough smile. "I thought I'd give you guys more room."

He snorted and took a long drag of his beer. "I don't need any room where you're concerned."

Everyone in the room grew silent, and she tried to play it off with a quick laugh and a smile. "Such a tease. Hey, look. They're back on the ice." That seemed to distract Roger well enough, which was a good thing since she'd had enough of him. She couldn't bear to look at Asher. Didn't want to know what he might be thinking.

Halfway into the third period, after watching the opposing team score enough goals to tie the game, their team finally shot one into the net. She jumped out of her seat like the rest of them.

"Ah, shit," Jeremy said as he wiped at his shirt. In his enthusiasm, he'd spilled beer down his shirt and onto the floor.

Zoe waved away his concern. "Let me get something to clean it up."

She hurried into the kitchen and pulled several paper towels off the roll. When she turned to head back, Roger blocked her way.

"Hey," she said with a smile as she attempted to slip past him, thinking he must be there for another beer.

He put an arm around her waist, capturing her. "What's your hurry?"

The scent of something stronger than beer wafted from his breath. It wasn't a stretch to assume he'd probably started drinking well before he'd arrived at their house. She pushed at him, trying to escape. "I need to get these to Jeremy. He's all wet."

Roger leaned close, burying his nose in her hair. "Do I make *you* all wet?" he whispered.

She tensed and shoved him, but he was much stronger than she was. "Let me go, Roger. You've had too much to drink and have obviously mistaken some friendly flirting as an invitation for something more."

He leaned back and looked at her. "I don't think so. I saw the way you looked at me. You want me, and I sure as hell want you."

What she needed was to yell for help, but she didn't want Asher to know the consequences of her flirting with Roger. He'd see it as her punishment, so instead, she narrowed her gaze. "Take your hands off me. *Right now.*"

She shoved against him, but her actions seemed to encourage him. When he covered her breast with his hand, the fear became real.

"Let me go," she growled and punched him.

"*Get off her.*" Asher's voice boomed through the kitchen as he strode into the room.

Roger looked up with a surprised expression only seconds

before Asher gripped his arm and jerked him away. Zoe escaped Roger's grasp as Jeremy rushed into the room.

Asher was angry enough that he looked like he could take down a mountain. "*Get the fuck out of my house.*"

Jeremy hurried forward to intervene. "It's cool, Asher. We'll go."

Roger stared down Asher until Jeremy reached him and tugged on his arm.

"You know what?" Roger allowed Jeremy to pull him away a few steps. "You're a real prick. You need to be knocked down a notch or two."

"If you think you're man enough to do it," Asher replied, his tone threateningly low.

"Stop. No." She couldn't stand by and let this come to blows. "Just go, Roger. Get him out of here, Jeremy."

She stepped between them, facing Asher, silently pleading with him.

Asher stared down at her as testosterone as thick as dense fog surrounded them. He shifted his gaze to Roger, and she sensed the tension mounting again.

"No," she said, taking Asher's hand, drawing his gaze to her. "Let them leave."

"Come on, dude," Jeremy said. "Let's go. We don't need the cops showing up tonight."

She prayed the sounds of shuffling behind her were Jeremy forcing Roger to leave. Every time Asher lifted his gaze, she squeezed his hand. After a few moments of Roger complaining and Jeremy cajoling, the front door slammed shut.

With the exception of the sportscaster's voice coming from the other room, the house was silent. She still held Asher's hand, and he still owned her with his gaze.

"I'm sorry," she whispered.

She tried to remove her hand, but he tightened his grip.

"What do you have to be sorry for? I'm the one who invited the asshole to our house."

The effects of leftover adrenaline left her shaking. "For watching the game and flirting with him. I should have gone to bed."

His barely contained raged flashed in his eyes. "No man has a right to put his hands on you unless you say so. Do you understand?"

She shivered and nodded.

"When I saw him touching you..."

He stopped and shook his head as though he couldn't continue without giving himself away.

She stared, trying to understand his meaning.

She couldn't have made him jealous. Not with him rejecting her time after time.

Her heart thundered as she dropped her gaze to his chin, needing a moment to get her bearings. After everything that had happened, she must be misinterpreting his words.

The intriguing curve of his lips caught her attention, and she indulged for a moment. Then, realizing the direction her thoughts had headed, she jerked her gaze back to his eyes.

Zoe found a seductive danger, potent as any narcotic burning there. Likely his leftover remnants from the altercation. Something hot and compelling left her helpless to do anything but stare. He'd entranced her with just a look.

She despised her attraction, but she couldn't move away. An insane part of her needed to know what would happen if she remained still.

Her breaths grew shorter as electricity charged between them. He eased closer to her, and she swallowed. Slowly, she tilted her gaze upward, nervous of what she'd see.

He still clasped her hand while he lifted his other and

placed it on her cheek. The look of longing and tenderness in his eyes was her undoing. "Zoe."

She closed her eyes as exquisite sensations fluttered in her chest.

"Look at me." His voice was deep and sexy, and stole what breath she had left.

She opened her eyes, and he searched her gaze for several seconds. She never could have imagined she'd find herself in that position, and she sure as hell couldn't understand what had changed.

He drew a roughened finger down her cheek and then tipped her chin higher with his thumb.

Oh, God...

This wasn't happening.

She couldn't kiss Asher Campbell.

His lips brushed hers with a soft touch, igniting a rare and fiery emotion inside her. Without thinking, she answered his kiss with one of her own, her lips lingering on his as she tasted the subtle flavor of cinnamon.

Overwhelming need flooded her, leaving her senseless, making her want nothing but his kiss.

He tilted his head as he deepened their kiss, and she opened for him. His tongue teased hers, swirling lust throughout her. She gripped his shirt as shivers of desire, of anticipation, erupted. *Sweet purgatory.*

Every spot where their bodies touched ignited and burned like dry kindling tossed onto a passionate fire. She wanted him. *Needed him.* "Asher," she whispered against his mouth.

She ran her hands up his chest, across strong shoulders, touching him in all the places she'd imagined over the past few days. Her fingers didn't come close to wrapping halfway around his biceps. The stubble on his jaw tickled her cheek. He molded her against him like they were meant to fit together.

She never would have thought it could happen. Never could have believed it.

But Asher was kissing her like she'd never been kissed, and she wondered if she'd hit her head and passed out and this was all a vivid dream.

Then he stopped. And straightened. Just like that, their kiss ended without warning. From the agonized look on his face, she could guarantee he wouldn't follow it with another.

With her breaths coming in pants, she met his gaze. "What's wrong?"

Heat blazed in his stormy eyes like a ship burning in the ocean. But he withheld his touch. "We can't do this."

The sting of rejection crushed her, stealing her voice.

He took another step back and released her hand, each movement a blast of cold winter wind to her heart. Had this been her punishment instead? And she'd fallen for it?

Oh, God. She wasn't sure she could bear the humiliation.

"I'm sorry. I shouldn't have taken advantage of the situation." He blinked a few times and then broke away from her.

Without a backward glance, he left her alone in the kitchen.

10

Zoe struggled to catch her breath, to make sense of what had just happened. As seconds ticked past, irritation chased away her shame.

Asher couldn't kiss her like that and then...*walk away*.

No. Not only no, but hell no. She would not let him belittle her again. Her self-esteem had taken enough beatings over the years from him. She wouldn't allow it any longer. She wasn't a toy, and this wasn't a game.

She stomped up the stairs, halting when she found his bedroom door closed. Like that would stop her.

She turned the knob and flung the door open, catching him unaware. He jerked his head upward at the intrusion and dropped the shirt he'd removed. The sight of him seated on the edge of the bed with all that muscle and skin gloriously exposed took her aback.

She hadn't considered knocking, hadn't considered what he might be doing behind his closed door.

He widened his eyes as she stared.

It was too late for common courtesy, so she inhaled a fortifying breath. "Just who the hell do you think you are?"

He blinked in surprise, seeming as baffled as she was by his earlier behavior. "Excuse me?"

She wasn't about to be swayed by a few meager words. Refusing to back down, she stepped farther into the room. "You don't get to do that to me anymore. You don't get to act like you like me and then shove it in my face when I decide to let you in. You've always enjoyed humiliating me, but it ends now."

Her breaths came heavier, heartened by adrenaline. But she'd done it. She'd stood up for herself, and it felt good. Damn good.

He stared at her for several long moments, confusion running rampant across his face. "I'm sorry. I don't know what you're talking about. I've never treated you that way."

No. That wouldn't work this time. He couldn't talk his way out of this one. She huffed. "Just admit it. Be a man and admit it."

He stood and walked closer, his palms out. "Zoe, I'm sorry. I don't understand what you're trying to say. I get I shouldn't have kissed you and then walked away, but I'm not ready for another relationship right now."

"*Relationship?*" She narrowed her eyes. "I'm not talking about a relationship."

He seemed genuinely puzzled. "Then what?"

"You, always humiliating me."

"I haven't." He shook his head as though searching his thoughts for answers. "Tell me when."

"Since the day we met." She listed off several incidents that popped into her mind, the sting of some still fresh in her memory. "Even now, every time we run in to each other, you say something snarky or rude. Why do you have to be so mean?"

He rifled his fingers through his hair. "Shit, Zoe. I wasn't being cruel."

She glared at him, stunned that he had the audacity to continue lying. "How can you say that?"

"Because it's true." He locked his gaze on her for a long moment, and she wondered what kind of lie he was concocting. "I don't mean to say those things, or at least I don't mean for my words to come out like they do sometimes."

She shook her head, not believing a word.

He opened his hands wide. "For some idiotic reason, whenever I'm near you, my words get messed up."

"Messed up?" Like he was messing with her mind right now?

"Because I like you, okay? I've always liked you, and you despise me."

His words echoed through her heart, through her mind. "You *like* me?" That was so not the answer she'd expected. And she couldn't believe it.

He shrugged.

She stared at him, stunned.

"What?" he asked after a few awkward seconds.

"I'm just waiting." And preparing herself. "Any minute, you're going to laugh and tell me it's a joke. I'm not going to be caught dead buying into your lies."

"They're not lies, Zoe. I've always liked you. You would know that, except you wouldn't give me the time of day."

She couldn't accept that something she'd believed for years wasn't true. "The only reason I wouldn't give you the time of day was because you were always so awful to me. I've had enough people in my life make fun of me. I didn't need one more."

"Aww...no, Zoe." He lifted a hand as though he wanted to touch her, but then let it drop. Instead, he took a step back, grabbed his discarded shirt, and pulled it over his head. "I know what you suffered through. I knew you couldn't help anything your mom did, even if others teased you about it. I would never want to add to that."

She shook her head as her universe spun. He was twisting things, trying to make her believe in an altered reality. She would have none of it. "That's not how it was. I specifically saw you stand back and watch Billy Hampton make fun of me. You were whispering along with the rest of them."

Asher gave her a reminiscent grin. "That part's true, but I wasn't whispering about you. I was telling Tyler that I was going to kick Billy's ass for harassing you so much. I don't know if you remember Billy's black eye a few days after that incident."

She widened her eyes as her mind resurrected the memory. She hadn't known how Billy had gotten it, but she remembered enjoying the sight of his injury. Felt karma had somehow given him what he'd deserved. "That was you?"

He nodded.

Her convictions slipped. "If that's true, then why didn't you say something at the time? Why let him bully me like that?"

"Trust me. I wanted to. Tyler made me wait. Said matters like that were best handled privately, without any witnesses. I agreed because I didn't want any backlash directed at you because I'd publicly humiliated him. Also, I didn't know if you'd appreciate a guy you barely knew and obviously disliked going to bat for you. Everyone would have been talking after that. I knew Billy wouldn't say anything if I handled matters in private because he'd have to admit I punched him if he did."

She blinked rapidly, trying to process the information as scars within her heart lightened without her consent. "If that's true, I would have considered you a knight in shining armor."

"Wish I would have known that." He snorted. "It's too bad how one wrong choice or a bit of misinformation can lead to years of other bad choices."

She searched his gaze, seeking his meaning as she tried to

regain her footing. "What do you mean?" Was he referring to their tumultuous non-relationship or something else?

He hesitated, indecision dancing in his eyes. "Nothing. Just, you know. If I hadn't always been so tongue-tied around you when we were younger...if I would have come to your rescue that day...who knows how things might have turned out?"

Her heart pounded faster, but she narrowed her eyes as though she hadn't understood his meaning. "Things between *us*?"

He smiled and shook his head as though to dispel whatever he'd been thinking. "Never mind. The past is the past. What happened, happened, and we are who we are today because of it. But I'm glad you know now. It's about time we cleared the air."

She swallowed, still unable to comprehend how wrong she might have been all these years. If what he said was true, what did that say about her as a person? She might be tempted to think she was as awful as her mother. Though he held some of the credit for the discord between them.

Time seemed to slow, and she couldn't form words to convey the thoughts tumbling through her mind. Could she have misread events? She didn't think so. But he seemed so... genuine with what he said. And the facts did mesh with his version of their story.

Even now, without him trying, humiliation unfurled inside her. Instead of spouting something appropriate or meaningful, all she could muster was, "Okay."

He stared at her as though he wanted her to say more, but she couldn't. Not now. Plenty had been said, and she needed time to process. He probably did, too.

Zoe turned from him, headed out the door and across the hall to her room. Once there, she softly closed the door behind her.

She didn't have time to compose a thought before it opened again. She whirled around in surprise, and Asher stepped inside, a determined expression on his face as he eliminated the short distance between them.

"That's it? That's all you have to say after I bared my soul. I think I deserve a response."

At that moment, he seemed so tall, his size intimidating. "You didn't exactly bare your soul. More like the soul of who you used to be, right? You just said we're not the same people anymore as we were back then. You've been married."

"Divorced," he added.

"I'm sure you no longer harbor those same feelings toward me." She carefully watched his eyes for a reaction.

He might have widened them the tiniest bit, but she couldn't be sure. "Yes, that's what I meant to say. We're no longer those people."

"Of course, we're not." She swallowed her unexpected disappointment. "Still, I'm sorry that I didn't know to thank you for your help all those years ago. Billy never bothered me after that, and I'd assumed he'd found someone else to harass."

"Good." A far too sexy smile lit on his lips. The same lips whose kiss had tempted her toward a dangerous outcome only moments earlier. "No apologies, okay?"

She lifted a questioning brow, trying to focus on what he'd said as opposed to the wild feelings buzzing inside her.

"It's crazy that we've lived this way for years," he continued. "I shouldn't have been looking if I wasn't man enough to talk to you."

How did she respond to that? Did she tell him it wasn't too late, that maybe they still had a chance?

He smiled. "I guess this means we have to be nice to each other from now on."

A smile blossomed in her heart. "I guess so."

"I'm sorry I kissed you downstairs. I should have done it ten years ago instead, before life intervened and ruined everything."

She wanted to touch her lips, to remember the feel of his kiss. "It's okay."

He nudged her arm with a soft fist. "It's too bad it took crazy Jenkins to get us to talk to each other. At least now we can be friends."

"Friends," she echoed as relief filled her. He wanted to be friends. She liked the sound of that. The animosity between them had been a source of discomfort for so long, and she was damn grateful to have it gone.

She slid a sideways glance toward him, trying to pretend his proximity didn't stir the longings inside her. *He'd always liked her?* How did she not know that?

"Is this where I get the gratitude lecture?" she said with a laugh. "We should be thankful he ripped us off because it brought us together? Not together, together," she was quick to add. "Just...you know what I mean."

"Maybe so." He met her gaze and held it. Flecks of silver radiated from his eyes and shot her with arrows of lost opportunities. "At least the rest of our time together won't be so miserable."

"Miserable?" she said with mock indignation, using humor to bury her true feelings. "I haven't made you miserable. You're the one who invited over the sexist molester."

The mirth disappeared from his face. "I am really sorry about that. I had no idea Jeremy hung out with assholes like Roger."

She nodded in appreciation. "And I'm sorry I flirted with him to piss you off."

He nailed her with a half-kidding, half-demanding gaze. "Is that what you were doing?"

She shrugged and then smiled.

"I won't bother bringing up Kiley," he offered in return.

"Kiley?" she managed to eek out.

"Yeah." He gave her a knowing smile. "I'll let you get to bed now, Zoe."

Compelled by unknown forces, she wrapped her arms around his neck and pulled him close. She wondered if she'd made a mistake, but he returned her embrace. "I'm glad we can be friends."

She had a second to savor his touch before he pulled away.

"Night, Asher," she said as he turned.

"Night, Zo."

After he shut the door behind him, she plopped on her bed with the distinct feeling life had tipped her on her head. Only time would tell how far.

11

Zoe woke the next morning, certain she'd tossed the entire night. Living with Asher had made one thing very apparent. Enemies, friends, or otherwise, she wasn't likely to get much sleep inhabiting the same space as that man. He was a force she'd never been able to ignore. More so now that she knew he'd been attracted to her.

As the night hours had droned on, she'd replayed the previous evening. She realized he'd always spoken of her in the past tense when he talked about his feelings. He'd once liked her, once cared.

She couldn't be certain if he did any longer. Obviously, he wanted to be friends, but that might be the extent of his current interest.

Was there anything she could do to change things? Did she even want to?

Normally, she would have stayed in her room until Asher had departed for work, but her heart urged her to glance into his beautiful eyes to discover if something beyond friendship still lingered there. If it did, then what?

She found him in the kitchen eating a bowl of cereal, lost

deep in thought, while he stood next to the sink. He'd dressed in a pair of ripped jeans and an old t-shirt that had once been a shade of blue. His biceps snagged her attention as they flexed when he lifted the spoon to his mouth.

He caught sight of her a second later, and his mouth curved into a grin that melted her insides into a puddle of lust, happiness, and incredible longing. She knew her expression mimicked his. Knew she'd probably given away more than she wanted to, but she couldn't help it.

"Morning." His deep voice rumbled through the quiet kitchen, fueling her hunger.

"Good morning." She pushed her hair back from her face, suddenly conscious of how disheveled she must look. She walked in and grabbed a coffee cup from the cupboard, keeping her eye on him, if only in her peripheral view.

"You're up early." He shoveled another bite into his mouth as she poured her drink.

"I couldn't sleep," she said, and then immediately wished she hadn't. She didn't want him thinking he'd kept her awake. "Too much caffeine last night, I think."

He frowned. "Weren't you drinking beer?"

Her cheeks heated as she realized her faux pas, and she shrugged. "That's right. Maybe it was the beer then."

With her nerves twisting, she took her cup to the table and sat, unable to keep from glancing at him again. He watched her, and the look he gave her set her blood boiling even more. He might not have bared his soul completely the night before, because she was damn sure interest still burned in his eyes.

He glanced at the clock on the wall, a remnant left by Jenkins, and took one last bite before dumping the remaining contents into the sink. He had another sip of coffee and then poured the rest into a thermos waiting on the counter.

With hurried footsteps, he crossed to the fridge, pulled out a yogurt and an apple, and tossed them into a lunchbox. Then he strode closer to the table where she sat and where his work boots waited.

"Is that all you're taking for lunch?" Maybe those were snacks, and he and Seth would head to town to eat.

"Running late," he said as he stuffed a socked foot into his boot.

But he worked so hard all day. That small amount of food wouldn't tide him over. "I could hurry and make you a sandwich. I have tuna."

"Thanks. That's nice of you to offer." He tied the laces on his second boot. "But I don't have time. I'm already late as it is. I'll figure out something later."

"Okay." She wanted to argue, but didn't.

He grabbed his bag and then paused before he strode from the room. "You look really great, you know?"

Before she could come up with a suitable response, he headed out the door.

With her heart thundering in her chest, she sat motionless until she heard his truck pull away. She didn't look great. She looked like a hot mess. Her hair always half-escaped the band she secured it with the night before. She didn't have on a hint of makeup, and the oversized shirt she wore as a nightgown had seen better days.

When she climbed the stairs to shower, she stopped in front of a mirror and tried to see what he had. She couldn't, of course. But that didn't mean his words didn't leave warm rays of sunshine burning into her heart.

———

Zoe sat at her desk in City Hall, staring toward the opposing wall in her small office, with thoughts of her recent interactions with Asher on auto reply. The sight of Noelle peeking into her office jolted her.

Noelle sent her a bright smile. "Hey! Can you sneak away for a walk?"

She glanced back to the quarterly payroll reports she'd been preparing for the town and then to the clock. It was shortly past eleven already, and she'd barely made a dent in her work. "Um, sure. Let me finish totaling this column and switch shoes."

Her friend fell into the chair opposite her desk, looking fresh faced with her blond curls pulled into a ponytail. She remained quiet until Zoe swiveled in her chair to pull the athletic shoes from beneath her credenza.

"What happened last night? With you and Asher?" Excitement clung to the edges of her words, coaxing Zoe's anxieties to life.

"What do you mean?"

"April told me Asher invited some rowdy friends over, but apparently Seth left before the evening ended. He mentioned, however, that you'd been flirting with one of Asher's friends, and Asher didn't seem too happy about it."

Zoe snorted as she stood and headed out of her office. "Seth left early and missed the disaster."

She'd learned long ago people would talk, and it was better to go with the flow than get upset. She tried to keep her own gossiping to a minimum, though, and she was cautious of passing along information that would hurt anyone.

Noelle's eyes grew wide as the two of them descended the city hall's steps. "What happened?"

The day had heated to warmer than Zoe preferred, but she appreciated the opportunity to get up and move as they talked. "Seth left just as Jeremy's friend, not Asher's, revealed his complete ability to be an asshole."

"Roger somebody, right?" Noelle asked. "I don't think I know him."

"Me, either. He must live in Pinecone, or he's new to town. I've never seen him before." Zoe turned and headed for the empty lot that the city often used for festivals and fairs. Large oaks surrounded the perimeter and would give them plenty of shade for walking. "He was cute until he started spouting some stupid male superiority rhetoric. That right there killed any interest I had."

Noelle rolled her eyes. "Why are guys such jerks?"

"Right?" Zoe agreed. "But that's not the best part."

"There's more?" Noelle grinned. "Do tell."

"Roger trapped me in the kitchen and tried to force himself on me, and Asher came to my rescue. For several intense moments, I was sure they'd come to blows. Roger was drunk beyond reason, and I've never seen Asher so angry."

Noelle surprised her by widening her eyes into a happy expression. "Angry because he didn't want another man to touch you. I see where this is going."

She couldn't say Asher's exact motives, but she was grateful he'd entered the kitchen when he had. "That's not the worst. Asher kissed me."

The world seemed to pause and inhale a sharp breath, just like it had the previous evening when he'd pressed his lips against hers.

Noelle stopped in her tracks and reached out a hand to halt her, too. "*He what?*"

She shook her head at the absurdity of it. "After Roger left. Asher was still angry over what the jerk had done. Testosterone was running high, and he...kissed me. It just sort of happened."

Noelle put her hands on her hips and eyed Zoe with a penetrating look. "That's wild, lady. But the most important question is, did you slap his face or kiss him back?"

Her cheeks heated as she considered Noelle's question. "I kissed him back, of course. Have you seen the guy?" She chuckled, trying to play off the interaction as no big deal.

Noelle blinked several times in disbelief. "Did hell freeze over last night and no one told me?"

Zoe angled an elbow toward Noelle but missed. "Hush."

Her friend glanced toward Rumors. "Wait until April hears this."

Years' old mortification reared its ugly head, and she gripped Noelle's arm. "You can't tell anyone."

Noelle tilted her head, perplexed. "Why not?"

"Because..." She paused as the events following their kiss replayed in her mind. "It didn't end well...exactly."

Her friend leaned in. "I thought you kissed him back."

"I did." She hated to admit that she wished she could turn around and do it again.

Noelle linked her arm through Zoe's and tugged her toward a park bench. "If we keep walking while you're talking, I'm going to trip. I can't keep my mind on my feet with what you're telling me."

Zoe exhaled a heavy sigh and reluctantly dropped next to her friend. "He kissed me. Then he changed his mind. I guess. I don't know." She went on to describe what had taken place.

Zoe shrugged. "So it ended with him telling me he'd always liked me, and I hadn't realized his attention stemmed from interest."

Noelle clapped her hands together. "This is so perfect! Now Seth and April, me and Kade, and you and Asher can all do couple things together."

Zoe hated to burst her bubble. "You didn't hear me. He always *liked* me. Not present tense. After he kissed me, he apologized, said he wasn't ready for anything like that." She paused as the truth rang like bells in her head. He might have seemed interested that morning, but he'd regretted kissing her the night before. "It's something to do with his divorce."

Her friend's shoulders slumped. "You think he's not ready?"

She had zero idea if either of them was ready for a relationship. Asher had only offered to be friends, and her gut told her that was the best outcome. "It hasn't been very long."

Noelle shrugged. "He's dated other women."

Her comment pinched. "He has?" Then why push her away? Unless his infatuation was a relic of the past.

Her friend chewed her bottom lip. "Perhaps I should ask April to question Seth further."

Zoe waved her hands wildly between them. "No, please don't. I just want to let things be. We're stuck living together for the foreseeable future, and peaceful companionship is my best option."

Noelle arched a brow. "Even if he's, as you said, really hot?"

She smiled at her friend's teasing remark. "Even then." There was no need to look further. No need to make life more complicated. She had enough to worry about wondering if she'd have a house in the future.

12

Zoe made an extra effort to be kind to Asher during the following weeks *and* to give him plenty of space. It was the least she could do. Technically, they were both at fault for the unfortunate years of misunderstanding and hostility. But she'd been the one to hold on and keep perpetuating the situation for such a long time. She should have listened to Noelle, but sometimes it was so hard to let go of past hurts.

They'd received no news from Jenkins, which she considered good news for her. At least for now.

She also did her best to keep secret her appreciation of him during different times of the day. Like when she wanted to hug him good morning or cuddle against him when they watched a movie at night. Or worse, how hot he looked right after a shower, with his hair still wet and the scent of a sexy ocean breeze hovering in his wake.

Time and again, she'd close her eyes as that smell drifted over her senses, and she'd remember the taste of him on her lips.

During the long days of summer, Asher worked later and

later, using every bit of sunlight to cash in on the pleasant weather to prepare for the lean times he'd experience during the winter. She never thought she'd feel bad for the guy, but she did. She'd never met a person who worked so hard.

To make matters worse, she'd heard from Noelle, who'd heard from April, that Asher and Seth had broken a water main when they'd been digging that day. That meant they'd be working late into the night to get things back on track.

Hence the reason she'd just packed up the leftover chicken pot pie she'd made for dinner. Many hours would pass before he or Seth would have time to eat if she didn't take them something. It was already past six, and she guessed they'd be working at least two more hours? Possibly three or four. Far too long for men who worked so hard. It wouldn't take her long to drive out and deliver dinner to them.

Not that Asher had given her the right to care, but she did. In fact, he'd done his best during the past few weeks to keep things between them friendly, but not too friendly, and she'd respected that. She and Asher reminded her of a couple who'd been married a long time and who'd become very set in their routines. They were considerate of each other, but lacked the passion she craved.

As the setting sun cast streaks of orange and pink across the western sky, Zoe turned off the main road near the center of town, and onto the dirt roads of a partially built subdivision. The first such thing in Aspen. Until now, most houses had lined the main road or occasionally sat back in the trees, but nothing in a little cluster like this.

It appeared as though they'd mostly finished one house, and two others were bare skeletons constructed of wood. She spotted Asher's truck and a red sedan near the farthest house and parked behind them, not far from a large tractor and a big hole in the road surrounded by mud. Unsure of where the men would want to eat, she left the food in the car.

As she neared the unfinished structure, hoping to find Asher inside, loud, arguing voices bellowed out. She immediately halted in her tracks.

"I don't give a shit." Asher's voice echoed with anger. "You owe me for my portion of the house, and you need to pay. Take out a loan. Sell it. I don't care."

She realized he was talking to his ex-wife, Dana.

"We're working on refinancing," Dana said, her words harsh. "But Tom's having problems with his credit. I don't know why you can't wait a few months."

"Great." A sarcastic laugh rolled out of Asher. "You left me for that?"

Pain ricocheted from his words and slammed Zoe, leaving her aching for him.

"We're not talking about Tom," Dana insisted.

"Fine. Then know this. At any moment in time, I might not have a place to live, and I need the money. Why the hell should I suffer? You're the one who cheated. Give me one reason you two should sleep in my bed, in my house, while I'm on the streets."

Oh, shit. This was not good. Zoe swiveled on her heels and retraced her steps. She'd obviously picked a terrible time to show up unannounced, and she absolutely did not want to be in the middle of that firestorm.

"Screw you," his ex-wife yelled.

Asher scoffed. "Grow up, Dana. You made your choices, so don't complain about the consequences."

She had almost reached her car when sobbing came from behind her. She glanced over her shoulder as Asher's ex-wife stormed from the house, her face streaked with tears. Dana took one look at Zoe and made a beeline for her car.

Zoe hesitated, not wanting to leave at the same time as

Dana, and certainly not wanting to step into the street as she revved her engine. Dana pulled forward, making a three-point turn in the middle of the unpaved road before she tore off, leaving a trail of dust to choke Zoe.

Divorce was a nasty business, for sure.

When quiet descended and the dust settled, Zoe walked around the front of her car and reached for her door handle. As she tugged on it, Asher emerged from the house. He stopped short, and she felt as though he'd busted her for doing something illegal.

She couldn't very well get in her car and leave at that point, but she didn't relish the upcoming conversation. "Hey," she said to him. Slowly, she headed in his direction once again.

He stepped off the slab of cement that would one day be someone's front porch and strode toward her.

"What are you doing here?" he asked in a much quieter voice than he'd used moments ago. "Did the sheriff's department call with news about Jenkins?" From the look on his face, he obviously expected the worst.

"No," she said as she reached him. "No news. Well, Milo did get a tip that someone said he'd seen a man fitting Jenkins' description in Vegas, so Milo's contacting that police department. But nothing concrete."

Anger and a touch of sadness lingered in his eyes. "I guess that's good news." He shrugged. "At least I'm not homeless and penniless yet."

The disheartened look on his face left her yearning to hug him better, but she resisted. "Maybe that won't happen. Maybe they'll find Jenkins."

He stared at her for a long moment, as though her expression provided an answer. "So, what's up then? Why did you drive all the way over here?"

She gave him a tentative smile. Suddenly, the idea of

bringing him dinner seemed awkward at best. "I'd heard you and Seth would be working late, and I figured you'd both be hungry."

His expression brightened by degrees. "You brought me food?"

"Just the leftovers from dinner." That she'd cheered him up left her feeling warm inside. She nodded toward her car and walked in that direction. He followed.

"Where's Seth?" she asked as she opened the passenger door and pulled out the box she'd packed.

"He left a while ago. Had to pick up his son from a friend's house. I guess April couldn't get back from Pinecone in time, but he'll be back." Asher eyed the contents of the box, his excitement contagious. "What did you bring?"

Her heart squeezed, making it hard to breathe. "Chicken pot pie and chocolate chip cookies. Bottles of iced tea." She passed the box to him, not knowing where he'd want to eat.

"Pot pie? Oh, God. That's my favorite. Thank you so much."

She prayed he wouldn't notice how desperately happy he'd made her. "Okay, good. I'm glad."

She glanced toward the driver's seat in her car and then back at him. "I guess I'll see you in a while, then. Don't forget to bring back the dishes. We don't have many."

He frowned. "You're not staying?"

His request surprised her, sending her pulse racing, but she couldn't deny she'd rather stay than go home to an empty house.. "I can, if you'd like."

Asher met her gaze. "I could use the company."

His gray eyes shackled her heart, creating an intangible connection that bound her to him. "Okay, sure." She kept her reply casual, while her insides danced to the beat of her heart.

13

"Watch your toes," Asher said as he led Zoe to the porch. "A construction site is not the safest place to walk around in sandals."

But he decided they sure looked good, along with the faded denim shorts that showcased her lovely legs and nice ass way better than the modest skirts and pants she wore to work. Her black tank displayed just enough cleavage to whet his appetite without giving away too much.

He preferred her this way. A little wild and untamed, with her loose, blond curls dancing about her bare shoulders. It was as though she set the true Zoe free after work and on weekends, and he was the only one lucky enough to see the authentic version of her.

Damn his ever-cursed luck. There was nothing worse than finding the right person at the wrong time. Why couldn't they have discovered and solved their differences years ago? He never would have looked at Dana if he'd believed he had a chance with Zoe.

But those weren't the cards fate had dealt him. They'd

offered up Dana, and he'd accepted. The result was a devastated heart in much need of repair.

Life could be a harsh teacher. Sometimes, it changed people into someone they didn't recognize. And who knew, maybe in the long run, he and Zoe would have ended up the same as he and Dana. One thing he knew for sure was loving and losing Zoe would have ended him.

He glanced over his shoulder and smiled to see her so close behind him. Maybe they'd always been meant to be friends. Good friends. Many times over the past few weeks, he'd considered seeing if she was interested in changing their status to friends with benefits. The urge to hold her and love her was a tough beast to tame, but sleeping with her wouldn't be fair to her when he had no intention of taking things further.

"Mind if we sit on the porch?" he asked.

"Sounds good." She smiled, and the achingly familiar longing gripped him once again.

Finding her outside after the difficult altercation with his ex had taken him completely by surprise. In a good way. Zoe's presence was a soothing balm to his wounded spirit. He wished he could tell her how much it meant to him that she cared. Dana had done nothing like that for him. Sure, she used to save him dinner, but she'd never gone out of her way to bring him anything.

He sat, and Zoe found a spot next to him. The scent of her sexy, flowery perfume caught his attention, and he inhaled deeper, taking all that was her into the depths of his lungs. He envied the curls that caressed her shoulders and the pillows she snuggled at night.

Unfortunately, he didn't know when or if he could give her what she deserved, so he wouldn't climb into that bed.

Instead, he lifted one of the plastic containers and then

fished a fork from the box. "Damn. My mouth is watering already. Seth really missed out."

She gave a dismissive laugh, but he could see that she was pleased. She shifted and leaned against a sheet of plywood that he'd soon cover with siding as she gazed across the green fields in the distance. "Don't you love this view?"

He snuck a sideways glance at her as he ate. She'd always been the most beautiful girl in the world. "I do."

And he had to stop thinking thoughts like that.

He tried to bury his attraction by focusing on his dinner, but his mind wouldn't slow. He'd once thought Dana could make him forget Zoe. Dana had been present and willing to love him, while Zoe had always been distant and unreachable. Now the tides had turned, but he was still just as lost in the underbrush.

"Have you ever considered leaving Aspen?" she asked, disturbing his thoughts.

He used the napkin she'd packed and wiped his mouth. "Not until recently."

"Me, either. It's too pretty here, and I love the quiet. A big city would suffocate me. But you think you might at some point?"

He nodded. "If I left, I'd find another small town somewhere close enough I could still drive to visit family, but far enough so that I didn't have to see certain people."

She turned her unforgettable brown-eyed gaze in his direction. "Meaning Dana?"

"Yep." The one person he didn't want to think about or talk about. He shoved another bite into his mouth. "Did I mention this is amazing?"

She chuckled. "You did."

The tranquility of the evening settled around them before she spoke again.

"I have to confess," she said softly. "I overheard the two of you fighting. I didn't mean to. I thought her car was Seth's, and I was outside the door before I heard the yelling."

He glanced at her, but she'd focused on the dirt mound in front of them. Dammit. "I'm sorry you had to hear that. It definitely wasn't one of my better moments." He'd let Dana push his buttons hard enough to turn everything red. Something he needed to watch in the future. Dana had hurt him, but he was determined those wounds wouldn't remain open forever.

Zoe caught his gaze then, hers full of sincerity. "It's okay. I understand how hard it must be for you right now, and I'm sorry for that."

"Life goes on." He'd make sure of it. "Besides, who wants to be married to an unfaithful woman, anyway? If I could just figure out this crap with our house, I'd be in a good position."

She sighed. "Right? Still, life goes on."

Indeed. Of all the people he'd known, she would understand that best. It sometimes amazed him Zoe hadn't turned to drugs or sex as an escape like her mother had. With the circumstances of her upbringing, he wouldn't have blamed her. "Ever hear from your mom?"

She jerked her gaze toward him, caught what he hoped she'd see as a caring expression, and then turned back toward the horizon. "No."

"How long has it been?"

She twisted her fingers together in her lap like she always did when she was uncomfortable.

He put a hand over hers, stilling her movements. "I'm sorry. I didn't mean to pry."

She lifted a shoulder and let it drop. "It's okay. I try not to think about her these days. Sometimes I wonder if I should try to track her down, to make sure she's still alive, but…"

"But that would open old wounds, and no one wants to do that."

"Yes." She blew out a deep breath. "As much as I would like to connect, to gain the mother I never had, I have to remind myself that's a childhood dream. She left me. No one made her. The mother I'd like to find doesn't exist."

He squeezed her hand before letting go. "Cookie? It's good for your soul." He opened the bag, secured one, and lifted the treat to her mouth.

She stared at him for a long moment, and he recognized the searching look in her eyes. She wondered if she could trust him, too. Then she took a bite of the cookie he held, dropping crumbs over the front of her shirt.

"Oops," he said and wiped the backs of his knuckles across her breast. Then stopped. "Sorry, I..."

"No worries." She smiled and cleared away the rest of the crumbs.

No worries, maybe, but his mistake had sent his thoughts roaring down the wrong road again.

She turned more fully to him, sending her blond hair swinging over her shoulder and making him wish he could twist the silky strands around his fingers. "We should make an agreement."

Her hopeful gaze ensnared him.

"No matter what happens, no matter who ends up with our house, let's promise we won't hate each other. After all this, that would be the worst thing ever."

He agreed, hoping she meant it.

"Good." She smiled. "We've spent enough of our lives not being friends."

"Absolutely." He finished eating, put the lid back on the container, and dropped that and his fork into the cardboard box. "Okay if I take two of those iced teas, along with the rest of the cookies, for later?"

"Of course. I brought them for you."

He set the box aside and stood before holding out a hand for her. She laid her fingers across his, and he helped her to her feet.

Could she really be capable of plotting to run him out of their house? It was hard to believe staring into those endless brown eyes. "If you wouldn't mind taking home the other serving you brought for Seth, I'll eat it later, too. Pretty sure I'll be hungry again when I get home."

"No problem." She studied his gaze, hers leaving him all tight inside.

"I need to get back to work if I'm going to finish what I need to tonight." As much as he hated to send her on her way.

"Yeah. Sorry." She took an awkward step away from him. "I probably stayed too long. But if I go home, I'll have to do the dishes because my roommate works late hours and doesn't have time to help."

"Ouch." He laughed. "How about this? He promises he'll do chores all weekend to make up for it." He grinned and reveled in the quick, but dangerous hit of electricity running between them.

Interest sparkled in her eyes. "Good, because that brings me to the other reason I wanted to see you. I want to give Noelle a bridal shower barbecue at the house and thought I should give you a heads-up that I'll have a bunch of people over."

"Sounds fun. Just the girls?" Appreciation for her thoughtfulness warmed him. He hated to keep comparing her to his ex, but once again, Zoe surpassed Dana by miles.

"I was going to invite the guys, too."

"Does that mean I get to come?" He needed to stop flirting with her, but she made it so easy. Plus, he loved the idea of playing host at his new house to his friends.

She glanced once again at the dirt piled in front of them. Ever since he'd kissed her, they'd played this baffling game of cat and mouse. She danced along the edges of flirtation as long as he didn't return the gesture. But the second he did, she shied away from intimate conversation.

It was a dangerous but enticing game. He shouldn't, but he loved any amount of attention from her. He could only guess she backed off in order to respect his wishes to keep it friends only, but her interest was obvious, and at times, his reasons faded like the setting sun.

"Would you really like to join us?" She acted as though he might turn her down.

"I'd love to, Zoe."

She met his gaze.

He was beyond tempted to take her hand, to caress her skin and see how soft she was, but doing so was stepping into tenuous territory. "Most of your friends are my friends, and it sounds like a great time."

A smile slid across her lovely lips. "I'd like that, too."

The knife of unfulfilled needs slashed him again. "Thank you for tonight. I needed this more than you'll ever know."

Was he stupid for keeping her out of his heart and life? Maybe she *was* the one for him. Maybe she always had been. If he could put his past behind him, he might see the future more clearly.

Unfortunately, time was more an enemy than a friend in this case, and he had as much control over that as his life.

Her blush stole a piece of his soul. "It's no big deal."

"It's a big deal to me." He needed her to know that. He stepped toward her and held her shoulders, intending to give her a quick peck on the cheek.

But as he bent closer, she turned to look at him, and his lips brushed hers instead.

Soft. Sweet.

After that, he was lost, and there would be no saving him. He savored her taste, knowing he shouldn't. His subconscious warned him, telling him to stop, but he couldn't let her go. Not yet. That would be like asking a homeless man to give up the hundred dollars he suddenly found in his pocket.

Asher slipped his hands down her arms and then pulled her tightly against his chest. She complied willingly, allowing him to take what he wanted more than the beat of his own heart. Spurred on by the fiery blood pulsing through his body, he teased her tongue with his, torturing himself all the while because he knew he wouldn't take it any further.

When she slid a hand up his chest, her actions flooded him with a rush of need swifter than the river in spring. His better senses kicked to the highest notch, reining in his animalistic desires.

"Shit." He hissed as he ended the kiss and stepped back. The resulting confusion on her face bruised his heart, tearing him to shreds. "I'm so sorry, Zoe. God, you can hate me for that. I shouldn't have..."

She held up a hand. Pain vied for the top position in her expression as she blinked in rapid succession. "Don't, Asher. Don't apologize." She took another step away from him. "It's okay. It happened." She bent to retrieve the box.

"It doesn't mean anything," she said when she straightened, but he could see the unshed tears in her eyes. "It was just a kiss. Nothing to freak out over."

He had to stop hurting her. "Zoe..."

She laughed, but her merriment echoed with the hollowness of an empty well. "Really. It's fine. You don't need to explain to me again."

He was an utter ass. "I know, but I feel bad. I just can't get mixed up with someone right now. I fell in love once and got burned, and I don't know if or when I'd want to try again."

Embarrassed anguish crossed her face, and she thumbed toward her car. "I'm going to get started on those dishes, and by the time you get home, we will have forgotten it ever happened. Okay?"

What could he say? He'd made things damn uncomfortable between them, and he had to allow her this out. "Okay."

She nodded once and turned toward her car.

"Thank you again for dinner," he called out.

She waved, but didn't look at him again as she got in her car and drove away.

"Dammit," he whispered as he adjusted the ball cap on his head. He apparently had a great knack for making women feel like shit. No wonder Dana had left him.

He ached to chase after Zoe or call her on the phone, but he couldn't. If he did, he would continue to lead her on.

Hell. He wasn't just an ass. He knew her life hadn't been easy, and he'd willingly made it harder. He was the greatest ass of all time.

———

Zoe kept her gaze locked on the road ahead and her wounded feelings barred behind the emotional equivalent of four inches of steel. If she cried, her tears meant he'd hurt her, and she couldn't accept that outcome. She had *not* let him into her heart that easily. To do so would be a foolish mistake, and she'd learned years ago not to be so careless around people.

She was strong and capable, and had no right to think Asher owed her anything other than friendship. She would be fine. She might be alone, but she'd be fine.

A shaky breath eased out of her, but her mind insisted on replaying the embarrassing scene again, chastising her as it did.

What the hell had she been thinking, showing up with dinner like she was Asher's wife or girlfriend? What had she expected the outcome to be? She couldn't blame Asher for the kiss. She was the one who'd put herself in the situation to begin with. She should have stayed home and minded her business.

Or, even if she had taken dinner to him as a friendly gesture with no strings attached, which she had to question now, she never should have stayed. She could have dropped off the food, left, and avoided her current predicament.

He was a lonely man, recently divorced, and she'd taken advantage of the situation to ease her own loneliness.

God, she was an idiot. One who would get her heart broken if she didn't do a better job protecting it. Asher had always been able to reach into the core of her and affect her. Even if his hurtful actions had never been intentional, she knew their power over her.

She needed to realign her thinking. They were friends. Finally. She didn't want to mess that up, especially not with them living together for an undetermined amount of time. And she sure as hell didn't want to fall in love with a man who didn't want her.

Talk about the perfect recipe for heartbreak.

She'd do exactly what she'd told him. She'd go home, do the dishes, and forget the incident ever happened.

14

The next morning, Asher pushed the two-by-four through the saw blade as the machine buzzed and screeched. When he was done, he lifted the wood and checked his cut. Good. Whichever one of his buddies had said they wouldn't need math after they'd graduated from school had lied. He used it every damn day.

Seth strode toward him carrying several more pieces of wood. "You're awfully quiet today. What's up? Have you been going the rounds with Zoe again?"

"Nope." Damned if he couldn't get the taste of her kiss off his lips, though. He'd tried to take her advice and pretend it hadn't happened, but that was as pointless as trying to stay dry when caught in a summer downpour. "Actually, we decided to be friends."

"*What...?*" Seth couldn't have looked more surprised.

Asher lifted his ball cap and wiped the sweat from his brow. The sun needed a few hours before it would be directly overhead, and already it rained miserable heat down on them. "I said we're friends. Neither of us wants to live in a house full of animosity, so we've called a truce."

More than a truce. Dammit. He'd come so close to caving to his baser instincts last night when he'd passed her in the hall before bed. She'd looked so sexy and warm and soft, perfect to cuddle up to after a long day's work. Luckily, she'd gone into her bedroom before he could make a move.

Seth nodded thoughtfully. "No more underhanded tactics? She might try to lull you into a sense of security, only to take advantage of the situation should everything go south."

He had to trust his gut. "Nah, I don't think so."

Seth eyed him, but said nothing as he laid the two-by-four on the table. Asher made the cut.

"How did this all come about?" Seth asked as he gathered the two smaller pieces of wood. "You guys have been enemies for years. I've seen the way she looks at you. If she was a blade, you'd be like this two-by-four."

"Turns out it was a misunderstanding. Several misunderstandings. She mistook my interest in her as me being mean to her because I screwed up everything I've said to her, and I never let her know how I felt."

"Really?" He didn't seem convinced. "Who holds a grudge for that many years over a misunderstanding?"

"Apparently, she did. It's hard to explain. It has a lot to do with her childhood, I think, but when I talked to her, it all made sense." Though when put to words without the emotion behind them, it sounded flat.

The skepticism remained on Seth's face. "Hmm...okay."

The need to defend her reared inside Asher. "You don't know her like I do. You don't know her well enough to judge her either way."

"And you do?" he challenged.

"I think I do." His words carried an emphatic edge. He shouldn't have to defend himself to his friend. "We've spent plenty of time together over the past few weeks. She's seen me at my worst, and I've watched her as well. She's sweet and thoughtful, and she doesn't go off like Dana used to."

"That's good." Seth gave him a nod of approval. "One point in her favor."

He couldn't believe his friend was being such a hardass. "She has other points in her favor, too. You need to know her better. She's throwing a party for Noelle and Kade, and she'll be inviting you. Then you'll see what I'm talking about."

Seth rolled his shoulders. "Look, dude. I'm on your side. I want what's best for you. You've been through a bad spell that might leave you vulnerable."

"Dammit, Seth. I'm not five. I can take care of myself. I know for a fact she's not trying to charm me. Or swindle me, or anything for that matter. We're friends."

His friend snorted. "How about seeing things from my point of view for a minute? She's hated you for years. When I say years, I mean *years*. She's gone out of her way to be rude to you, and why? You're a decent guy. Then, when the guys were all over to your house watching the game, she hit on that loser, Roger, like a whore on cocaine."

Asher straightened his chest as red flooded his vision. "You call her a whore one more time, and I'll knock you flat."

Seth was quick to hold up a hand. "Relax, man. I wasn't calling her a whore. I just wanted to get my point across. Like I said, I'm on your side."

"Then lay off, all right? Zoe's fine."

His friend lowered his voice before speaking again. "Have you fallen for her, man?"

"*What?*" He glared at Seth. "Where the hell are you coming up with this stuff? I'm not in love with her. After Dana, I don't have any plans to roll down that road for a damn long time."

Seth widened his eyes in surprise. "No need to take offense. Like I said, I'm only looking out for you."

Asher blew out a disgusted breath and adjusted his hat again. He needed to calm the hell down. It seemed everything had sent him over the edge lately.

Seth took the boards inside the unfinished house while Asher worked on cutting more. A few moments later, Seth was back. He fixed him with a serious look. "You're not sleeping with her, are you?"

Asher refused to get sucked in and riled up again. "No, I'm not sleeping with her, and I don't plan to." He kept his voice calm even though he now had Seth to thank for reviving the fantasy he'd indulged in for weeks.

"Good. That's good." He bundled more wood into his arms. "Don't sleep with her. That will only complicate things. If you can manage that, I guess you'll be fine."

Asher snorted. "You have nothing to worry about."

———

Noelle handed a warm cinnamon roll to Zoe. "I thought you said you wouldn't be coming in everyday anymore."

She groaned as usual as they walked to their regular table. "What can I say? I'm addicted. You're my crack dealer."

Noelle laughed. "I've never been called a crack dealer before."

"Yeah, well, it's about time, then. You have me so addicted I'll never stop. I'd give up gas and walk to work if I had to choose between the two." She pulled off a piece and shoved it in her mouth.

"I should put you on a billboard."

"Right?" Zoe grinned at her friend, trying to maintain the level of happiness she'd achieved after hours of hating herself the night before. "The homeless woman who survives by eating Rumors' famous cinnamon rolls."

Noelle chuckled. "You're not homeless."

She rolled her eyes and tried to smile. "Not yet."

Noelle's expression flipped to a look of concern. "What's wrong? Did you get some news?"

Zoe widened her smile to combat the turmoil rolling inside her. "No news."

"Then what?"

She shrugged. "Why do you think something is wrong?"

Noelle pinned her with a no-nonsense gaze. "I can see it in your face. Are you going to tell me, or are we going to sit here all day?"

She gave up trying to pretend happiness. "Nothing's wrong. But everything is. There's no news on the house, but is that good news or bad?"

Noelle tilted her head in thought. "No news is good news, right? As of right now, you still have your house, and you should save your worrying for when you have something to worry about."

Zoe stared at her friend, trying to decide if she should say something about Seth, which was silly because she desperately needed someone to talk to. "It's not just the house. I might need somewhere to stay until we get this figured out. I don't think I can live with Asher much longer."

Noelle lifted her brows. "Is he being a jerk again?"

"No. It's not that."

"He kissed you again?"

"It's worse than that." She needed to talk, needed to spill before she exploded, but this wasn't easy to admit. She inhaled and then slowly released her breath. "I think I like him," she whispered so no one would overhear.

Noelle choked on her coffee. "Excuse me?"

"Shh..." Zoe furtively gestured toward the other customers, and Noelle nodded her comprehension.

Although Noelle had the music in Rumors at a level that would drown out others' conversations, Earlene Smith sat only a table away, and Zoe didn't need the worst gossiper in Aspen telling everyone she came across.

"It's stupid. I know, okay?" Zoe kept her voice low. "He wants absolutely nothing to do with me. But I've gotten to know him, and I like him."

Happiness glowed in Noelle's eyes. "I just heard the best piece of gossip all year."

Zoe's stomach flipped, and she glanced over her shoulder at the old woman to make sure she wasn't listening. "Don't even tease me about that."

"You know I won't say anything." Noelle leaned in closer. "But really? You like him?"

"I'm so screwed. I didn't want to like him. But then it seemed easier to stay in the house together if we were friends. And being friends, we've talked, and I saw a different side of him."

Zoe shook her head as the truth of her feelings spilled like marbles across the floor. "If he and I both liked each other, it would solve an enormous problem over who is going to get the house. I looked at Asher's paperwork, and if I go by the dates listed, I think Jenkins sold it to him first. That means it belonged to him, so Jenkins shouldn't have sold it again to me, don't you think?"

Noelle grimaced. "That makes sense. Although you should consider which day Jenkins gave his verbal agreement to you. I'm not sure if that would help or not. In the end, a judge may have to decide. You might think about getting a lawyer, just in case."

The abrupt scraping of Earlene's chair on the tile floor interrupted their conversation, and Zoe glanced at her again. Luckily, the wrinkled old woman didn't look their way as she headed out the door.

"That woman always makes me nervous," Noelle said. "She has the nose of a bloodhound, and it wouldn't surprise me if she has a bionic hearing aid."

"No kidding." Zoe added. "She thinks knowing everything about everyone is her reason to exist, her contribution to society. One day, it will bite her in the ass."

"Yep. That big ol' karma bus will circle around and flatten her good." They both snickered at Noelle's remark.

Unfortunately, Zoe's torturous thoughts wouldn't let her off the hook for long, and an image of Asher's smile and the accompanying hurtful feelings from his rejection rushed back in. "Tell me what to do, Noelle. How do I unlike someone? How do I stop thinking about how sexy he is, whether he's in nothing but pants or covered in dirt from a hard day's work? He's probably all smelly, but I just want to put my hands on him."

Noelle chuckled. "Trust me, I understand a man being sexy when he's all dirty. Kade loves to work on cars, and he's so hot with grease on his hands and smudges on his face."

"See?" She wasn't crazy. "It must be built into our biology. You don't suppose they know we're attracted to that sort of thing, do you?"

Noelle laughed then. "No. I'm sure there are enough women who aren't turned on by that to keep the guys from learning our secret."

"Good." She inhaled in relief. "The last thing I want is for Asher to know how much I lust after him."

"Why? Maybe he has similar feelings, and it could be a good thing."

She shook her head vehemently as the sting of their most recent interaction steamrolled her again, leaving her with a twisting pain in her heart. "He doesn't. He's made it more than clear that he's not interested in anything like that with me. He kissed me twice, and both times, he immediately regretted it. He keeps telling me he's not ready for a relationship."

Noelle gave her a hopeful look. "He must like you somewhat if he's kissed you twice."

She'd considered that. "Or it's been a while since he's had sex, and he might have kissed any woman within range during a weak moment."

Her friend shook her head. "Any guy would be lucky to have you. Maybe he's still in love with his ex?"

Zoe shrugged, thinking it was unlikely after their recent interaction.

"But you think he truly doesn't like you?" Noelle prodded.

"I don't know. I wonder if maybe he's scared of getting hurt. Or maybe he just needs more time to heal."

"How long has it been?"

Zoe sighed. "They've been divorced for six months and separated five months before that."

"That's almost a year. Then again, there's no telling how long it takes. I can't say I blame him. You or I might feel the same way. But that does seem like a reasonable amount of time." Noelle lifted her coffee cup and drank. "Maybe you should flirt with him. If he's even mildly interested, you'll know."

She'd been over the same thoughts so many times that her head spun. "He's kissed me twice. He *must* be mildly interested."

"True." Noelle eyed her. "Maybe it is best if you leave things be. The answers you seek might not be the ones you want, and the last thing I want to see is you getting hurt."

Asher's comment about love being dangerous echoed back at her. "I just wish I knew if I should be patient and try to build something with him, or if I should focus my efforts on protecting my interests." As well as her heart.

"That is a tough one." Noelle stared at her thoughtfully. "If you like him, I'd say give him a chance and give him time. Protect yourself while you do. There's no reason to hurry."

"You're right." Except it might mean losing her sanity in the meantime. She exhaled a frustrated breath. "So, the pre-wedding barbeque. How about next Sunday?"

A happy smile lit Noelle's face. "Are you sure, Zoe? I had thought after all this mess you might not want to host it at your house."

"I'm more than sure. Asher's even on board and looking forward to it."

Noelle lifted her brows and gave Zoe a hopeful smile. "Well, that's good for now, so go with it. Worry about other things when and if the time comes."

Zoe nodded and dug deep, hoping to find a hidden reserve of patience. Maybe, if she waited long enough, he'd realize he wanted to try, too.

15

Zoe woke early on the day of Noelle and Kade's party. She'd left the kitchen a mess the night before, opting to get an early start in the morning when she wasn't so tired. That meant she had a full day's work ahead of her before the guests arrived and then plenty afterward.

The moment she left her bedroom, the amazing scent of fresh coffee wafted up to greet her. Her stomach rumbled, knowing breakfast would soon be on the way, and she smiled as she descended the stairs. Even if they were only friends, he was a hell of a cook, and no one could prevent her from enjoying that aspect.

Asher stood in front of the stove with a spatula in his hand. His hair was still rumpled from sleep, and he wore nothing but a pair of black boxer briefs. Powerful thighs tapered down to muscular calves, which had been honed from hours of physical labor. She widened her eyes, shocked that he wore so little.

Damn.

"That smells really good," she said as she stepped into the kitchen.

He startled and cursed. "You're always sneaking up on me."

"Sorry." She covered her smile with her hand. Her gaze dropped again of its own volition, and she quickly corrected herself.

He grinned. "I'd planned on putting on pants before I came up to wake you." Meaning he knew damn well what she'd been eyeing.

She shrugged as though she hadn't noticed his near naked-ness, and crossed her arms over her chest to shield her hard-ening nipples. "It doesn't bother me. I'm sure with living together, it's bound to happen."

He walked toward her with the spatula in hand, and her heart thudded like a bass drum. His cocky, confident stride sent her thoughts buzzing around her head like drunken bees. How was she supposed to hide her feelings when her own body betrayed her?

"Thanks for understanding," he said. "But I don't want to be disrespectful when a lady is present."

She swallowed as he held out the spatula. The only words that formed in her brain were objections to his comment. She didn't find him disrespectful at all. In fact, she highly appreci-ated the view.

"If you could finish the eggs, I'll be right back." His hand brushed hers as he passed off the utensil, leaving her with a multitude of relentless flutters.

She stayed rooted as she watched him walk away. Then she closed her eyes and inwardly groaned, knowing she'd never get the image of his well-defined butt and strong back out of her mind. Like ever.

"The eggs?"

His question brought her eyes wide open. She'd thought he'd left, but he still stood in the doorway.

"Yes," she said with a flourish and hurried toward the stove. She didn't miss his satisfied grin before he turned once again.

"Shit," she hissed the second he disappeared. She'd gawked at him like he was a male cover model showing all that skin for her delight. She was certain he'd caught sight of the lust burning inside her. How could he not? And now he knew she still wanted him.

Sick embarrassment rolled through her.

Worse, he'd made it clear nothing would happen between them. Even though he seemed to like the fact that she looked.

God, what a mixed-up mess they'd become entangled in.

He returned a few minutes later dressed in jeans and a t-shirt, which now made her pink nightgown seem out of place.

She shoveled eggs on to both of their plates and then turned to leave. "I should change, too."

He caught her arm right above the elbow, his strong fingers burning into her flesh. She tentatively glanced upward, nervous to see his expression. He towered a good eight inches above her, and all she could think was how powerful he seemed at that moment. And how badly she wanted him to kiss her again.

"You're fine." His deep voice rumbled through her as he dropped his gaze like she'd done with him. She inhaled a slow but steady breath, feeling exposed in her thin cotton gown.

"But you changed," she countered.

"But if you go now, your eggs will be cold by the time you return."

How could she argue with that? "Okay."

She slowly slipped from his grasp. When she glanced over her shoulder, she caught him watching her as she padded across the wood floor to the table. His obvious gaze left her uncertain and more than a little turned on. She sat, poured a glass of orange juice, and focused on that.

He took the seat across from her, leaving her directly in his line of sight. "You're beautiful without makeup."

Her heart jolted as though he'd shocked her with high

voltage cables. "Asher…" She blinked a few times, not knowing what to say. She couldn't stop her heart from soaking up his words even as she recognized the danger in doing so.

"Just say thank you," he said after a few moments.

Heat rushed up her cheeks, making everything much worse. "Thank you." As hard as she tried, she couldn't keep her smile from matching his. To save herself, she lifted a piece of bacon and stuffed it into her mouth.

She repeatedly redirected her focus to her food. Then every second or so, her brain would sneak in a thought of him. His seductive eyes. The amazing feel of his lips on hers. The rock-hard body she wanted to melt against.

She dared a glance at him and found him watching her with blatant interest, shining like a full moon on a cloudless summer night in the mountains. The sight of him watching her like that stole her breath.

It was a moment before she trusted herself enough to speak. "I'm surprised you're up so early." The statement was lame, but at least it was something.

He dipped his head. "I figured you could use the help today."

She hadn't had many people in her life she'd been able to rely on. "Thank you. That…means a lot."

"You didn't think I would let you do everything by yourself, did you? I live here. I can help." He held up a hand. "No, I *want* to help, okay?"

The thought of having someone to help carry her load over-whelmed her emotions. She blinked quickly to keep her silly tears at bay. She'd grown up always handling things on her own, so it seemed normal. But this? This was very nice. "I really appreciate that."

"Yard first while it's still cool outside?"

She nodded. "That would be great. Jenkins left a bunch of lawn chairs in the shed. I thought I'd pull them out."

"What about a table?"

She hadn't gotten that far. "Uh, I guess we need one. Maybe Kade has one we can use. I'll call Noelle."

"Don't worry about it. I'll take care of that. What else? The house is mostly clean. Do you need help with the cooking? I'm a decent cook."

That she knew. "I think I can handle the cooking for the most part."

"Okay. Let me know what I can do to help."

Her first thought was to ask him to kiss her and hug her. That would help so unbelievably much. But unfortunately, he hadn't been referring to physical affection.

———

As Asher and she spent the better part of the morning and early afternoon prepping for their party, Zoe's spirits soared. They worked well as a team. He was more than happy to do heavy lifting and reaching, and all the things that would have worn her ragged.

She hadn't realized how nice it was to have a man about the house.

Just before two, he popped into the kitchen, catching her snacking on the watermelon.

"Save some for the party," he teased as he strode closer to her.

"I had to make sure it was good," she said with a grin. "Can't serve tasteless watermelon."

He nodded toward the wedges she'd cut. "And?"

"It's so good. Best I've had in a long time. Want some? I cut up a few chunks." She pointed to the pile on the cutting board.

"Sure." He held up his dirty hands and opened his mouth.

It took a second for her to realize he wanted her to feed him. She swallowed. Okay... They were friends. Friends could do this.

She lifted a chunk and slipped it into his mouth. Her fingertips brushed his lips as she did, shooting her with intense shivers. He locked his gaze with hers as she licked the juice running down her forefinger.

Heat jumped between them, and she realized how her innocent act must have come across. He probably thought she was trying to seduce him at this very moment.

"Good, huh?" she said, hoping to diffuse the situation and any resulting thoughts he might have. She tore her gaze from him and moved to the sink to wash her hands before she finished up.

She couldn't look at him, couldn't stir those feelings inside her even more, only to have him push her away again. The rejection, however understandable, still hurt.

"It's excellent."

Sounds of a drawer sliding open echoed behind her, followed by the clanking of silverware. When she glanced back, she found him with a fork in his hand, stabbing another piece.

Why hadn't he done that in the first place?

She wiped her hands on the dishtowel before pulling the plastic wrap from another drawer. She approached him again in order to cover the watermelon slices, but she was careful to not make eye contact or come close enough she might accidentally touch him.

He stepped away, giving her space. "I'm going to get us a table if you're done with me for now."

God, she hadn't even started. Hadn't begun to use him how she wanted. "Yes. I can handle things from here on out. Thanks for all your help."

His boots clomped on the floor as he walked away, and she

dared a glance at his retreating form. As he reached the edge of the kitchen, he looked over his shoulder. A devastating smile curved his lips as the happiness in his eyes burned brighter. "We're going to have a great time tonight. I'm looking forward to it."

Her insides turned warm and mushy. She returned his smile, but worked hard to keep it slightly chilled. "We are."

Once he was gone, she mentally cursed herself. She wasn't sure how long she could hide her true feelings, not when she was around him and his gorgeous eyes and heavenly body so often. A girl could only ignore her impulses for so long.

Did he not realize how his actions tortured her? How charming he was just being himself? Any woman would be lucky to have him.

She was like a chained up chocolate addict in the middle of a candy factory. Temptation after temptation thrust in her face, and she could only look. No touching. No tasting.

Surely, anyone would go crazy before long.

16

Zoe caught sight of Asher briefly before the party as she exited the bathroom with a towel wrapped around her head and another around her body. He'd just reached the top of the stairs, and their gazes collided like two freight trains running full speed into each other.

"Hi," he said as he raked a deliberate gaze over her, leaving her feeling as though she didn't have a towel to shield her. Her thoughts quickly jumped to their first night together when he'd walked in on her while she was in the tub.

"Did you get the table?" she asked, to avoid the wild emotions churning inside her. He'd been gone for a couple of hours, and she'd been worried he wasn't having any luck. She should have prepared better, but she'd been more concerned with what she'd serve as opposed to where her friends would eat the meal.

"Got it. It's already in the backyard and everything is set up."

"Great." She held her towel tighter to her when his gaze dipped. "I'll go dry my hair then. Everything else is ready."

He brushed at the random wood shavings on his blue t-shirt

and pants. There was even a couple in his hair. "I'm going to grab a quick shower."

She didn't ask where the shavings had come from. Instead, she slipped inside her bedroom and shut the door, finding sanctuary away from his gaze. This meaningless flirtation had gone on for too long. Her heart and her self-esteem couldn't take much more.

If he liked her, then he needed to make a move. If not, then he needed to stop looking at her like he did. If he couldn't do that, then he should stay away as much as possible.

When she emerged forty minutes later with her hair and makeup done and dressed in a short black and white floral sundress, the bathroom door was open, as well as his bedroom door.

Certain he'd already showered and dressed, she hunted for him on the lower level and found him in the kitchen with a large metal tub full of ice. He buried a bottle of beer in the ice, followed by a bottle of water. Then a couple cans of soda and more beer.

"That's a great idea. Where did you get the tub?" she asked as she breezed into the room. She'd shored up her defenses once again while in the shower and had prepared to have a pleasant evening.

He looked up and paused with a beer in mid-air. "Wow. Don't you look nice?"

Unwanted heat radiated through her like a wildfire, and she shook her head in a friendly warning. She couldn't let him continue, or she'd never survive. "You have to stop being so sweet, or I'm going to think you're hitting on me."

He stared at her thoughtfully. "Would that be a bad thing?"

"Yes," she answered, even though she didn't want to. "Because then you'll kiss me again, and we both know how that ends." She pinned him with a look. He had to realize how unfair that was.

He nodded in agreement. "You're right. I apologize." The look he sent her was dutifully remorseful, and she hated every second.

She forced a reluctant smile and pretended her heart hadn't taken another hit. "I'm guessing people will start to arrive in fifteen minutes, so we should probably haul everything outside."

"Already on it." He lifted the heavy tub, his biceps bulging under the weight. She would have filled it outside so it wouldn't be so heavy, but he seemed to manage just fine.

"I'll get the door." She opened it for him and returned to grab the platter of skewered chicken kabobs. She passed him at the doorway as he reentered the house. The second she stepped outside, she stopped short.

"*Oh, my gosh.*" While she'd been busy inside for most of the day, he'd transformed their country backyard into a magical setting. Fat lightbulbs strung from tree to tree around the patio, while lively music echoed from an unseen speaker. He'd moved the garden tools off the cement. Leaves and other debris were completely gone, and in the center of the patio sat a beautiful redwood table. It was simple in structure. Wooden slats held together by other pieces of wood, but it was impressive all the same.

She turned to find him watching from the doorway. "How did you do this? And who agreed to lend you that beautiful table?"

"What can I say? I'm a construction guy. I know how to get shit done." From his smile, she could tell her reaction pleased him.

She arched her brow. "The table?"

"Made it."

Her mouth fell open before she could stop it. "*Today?*"

He shrugged. "A little sawing. A little screwing. It's not rocket science."

She wandered to the table and set her tray down. That he would go out of his way to make this so lovely touched her deeply and decimated any defenses she had left. She turned and caught the genuine smile on his lips. "Thanks for this. For everything."

His sentiment wrapped so tightly around her heart, and she was sure she'd never be free. How could she have once hated this thoughtful, far-too-handsome man?

"Just don't tell the guys I decorated." He winked.

She laughed. "You're going to make me look awfully good to my friends."

His expression sobered into a serious look that caused her heart to miss a beat. "You already look amazing, and I had nothing to do with that."

The lighthearted flirtatious butterflies in her stomach took flight, leaving her with a genuine fear of being hurt.

Had he changed his mind about her? About them? Or would she be sucked in one more time, only to be shut out again?

She looked at him with his beautiful eyes and powerful arms that she longed to hold her. Everything in her prompted her to walk straight up to him and kiss him and never stop.

But she couldn't. She wouldn't.

And she knew he wouldn't either.

"I already warned you. Stop being so nice," she said in a teasing voice, as she returned to the house, drowning out the uncertainty stampeding through her head. "Our guests will be here soon, so you'd better focus."

She brushed past him, her heart thumping like a flat tire on the freeway and didn't watch to see if he'd follow her inside. Instead, she went directly to the fridge again and pulled out the bowl of potato salad she'd made earlier. She grabbed the utensil basket in her other hand and headed outside again.

"Hey," Noelle said as she and Kade entered the backyard. She hurried forward and relieved Zoe of the salad. "This looks fantastic. All of it. Thank you so much for doing this for us."

A smile blossomed on her lips. "My pleasure. Asher helped me a ton."

"Yeah?" Noelle glanced over her shoulder at where Kade and Asher stood near the gate. "Tell me more," she said in a conspiratorial voice.

Zoe turned toward the house with a chuckle. "There's nothing more to tell. He was kind enough to help me. End of story. I need to bring out more stuff."

Noelle followed her inside. "I think you're wrong, Zoe. I saw the way he looked at you just now. He might not have made a move yet, but he's thinking about it."

She pulled the tray of watermelon from the fridge and set it on the counter harder than she'd intended. "I don't want him to. I don't want to wonder anymore if he likes me or not. If we have a chance or not. It's like being on this never ending, horribly wild roller coaster, and I'm done riding it."

Noelle put a hand on her forearm, her eyes full of concern. "Zoe?"

"I mean it. I'm done. He and I can be friends, but that's all it will ever be. When I think about the future in those terms, I feel okay. Disappointed, maybe. But okay. When I wonder if we might have a future together, life becomes crowded and crazy with my thoughts."

Zoe firmed up her emotions. "I don't know where I stand. I don't know what to do. Do I laugh with him, or is he going to wonder if I'm flirting and turn away from me? When I do my hair, I wonder if he'll like it. When I cook dinner, I think about him. He's invaded every damn second of my life, and he hasn't earned that right. He doesn't even want it." She released a sarcastic laugh. "I can't do this anymore. I've officially removed whatever offer might have been on the table."

Noelle put a comforting hand on her shoulder. "Oh, Zoe. I'm so sorry."

She forced a smile. "It's okay. It's better this way."

The door opened, and Zoe bent, using the shield of the fridge to gather her bearings.

"You guys okay?" Asher asked Noelle. "You've been in here awhile."

"We're great." Noelle lifted the watermelon and headed toward him, creating another barrier between them. "Take this out, and we'll be right there."

He chuckled. "Don't make me wait too long. Milo and Anna are here, and Milo said he has news."

Zoe stiffened and met his gaze. "He does?"

"Yes, but he said he'd wait for you."

She couldn't imagine what it might be. Unless it was information on their house. "Oh, God. Give me a second."

Asher left them alone, and Zoe did her best to take a calming breath. "I've got to get it together. I need to greet my guests, and shit, I'm ruining your party."

Noelle hugged her. "No, you're not."

She took solace for a few seconds and then straightened. "No more about me. Just you and Kade and Milo's news. I pray he's here to say they've found Jenkins."

They gathered the rest of the fixings and walked outside together. Milo and Anna greeted them, along with Seth and April.

Everyone hugged and laughed, and Zoe helped herself to a beer. It promised to be a long night, and she needed every ounce of help she could get.

Asher gave Milo a friendly punch to the arm. "Out with it, man. You've got news, and we're dying to hear it."

That Milo was telling the group during their party was a good sign. If it was bad news, he surely would have told them privately later on.

He inhaled a deep breath. "Authorities in Fort Worth say they have Robert Jenkins in custody."

17

Zoe sucked in a breath hard enough to draw everyone's attention, and she covered her mouth with a shaking hand.

Milo tipped his head as though to say, *you're welcome.*

"It's not a sighting?" Asher asked, his eyes full of hope. "They actually have him this time?"

Milo turned to him. "That's what they tell me. I'm waiting for a call from the sheriff to see if we want to send someone down to pick him up, or pay to have him brought back."

Zoe caught Asher's gaze, and the thought that one of them might move out soon was a slap of reality. Suddenly, she didn't want Jenkins to come back at all. She'd sworn she was done with Asher. But now, faced with the real possibility that they'd be able to get on with their lives separately, she wished it wasn't so.

Asher could walk out the door, and that might be her last shot to be close to him.

Asher's expression oozed with eagerness. "How soon will you know?"

Was it so bad, she wanted to ask, living there with her?

"Could be anytime," Milo responded. "I have my phone on me. Just waiting to hear."

"That's damn fine news," Seth said and clapped Milo on the back.

"We need to toast." April nudged her husband. "I'll have a soda."

Everyone at the party seemed thrilled as they gathered drinks and drew in a close circle. Asher lifted his beer. "To the Fort Worth PD and our own fine officers here in Aspen. Thank you so much."

The others raised their drinks and echoed his sentiments. Asher met Zoe's gaze with a smile that she felt obligated to return. She tipped her beer, but the liquid barely seeped down her constricted throat.

As she worked her way through helping Asher cook steaks, eating, and cleaning up, she kept her emotions locked deep inside. She'd just sat down at the table afterwards when Milo's phone rang. Conversations ceased, and all eyes turned to Milo.

"I'll get the music." Asher stood and dialed down the volume.

"Hey, Sheriff. Thanks for getting back to me." Milo paused for a moment while the sheriff talked, and Zoe strained to hear the muffled voice coming from his phone.

"Is that so? Are they sure?" He lifted his brows as though surprised. "Okay, then. I guess we go from there."

He hung up the phone and then shook his head. "Not our Jenkins, after all."

Asher came up out of his chair. "*What*?"

"Clerical error is what Reynolds said. They had a suspect by the same name and another man that looked similar to our Jenkins. Unfortunately, they were two different men, and neither was ours."

Kade put a hand on his shoulder. "Sorry, dude. Bad turn of events."

"Don't worry," Noelle added. "They'll find him. He's an old guy. How far can he get?"

Anna gave him a commiserating nod. "If anyone can find him, Asher, Milo will."

Asher focused on Zoe. "I'm sorry. I wish this would have been the answer for us."

She nodded and tried to mirror her expression after the others, but deep inside, she wanted to cry with relief. Thankfully, she wouldn't lose Asher so soon. Unfortunately, she still didn't know where she stood with him, which meant the back-and-forth stress would continue.

She inhaled a fortifying breath. "Let's not let it ruin the party. It's not like we've been robbed again. Everything is still the same as it was this morning. The police are looking. Milo won't let it drop, and we just have to be patient."

"She's right," Asher said. "I still have a roof over my head. I have great friends and a great job. I can't say I have much to complain about." He turned the music up.

Milo stood and held out a hand to his wife. "I say we dance."

Anna laughed and rolled her eyes. "Every chance you get."

"That's right, darling." He twirled her and caught her again in his embrace.

After that song, Milo dragged Zoe away from the table, and soon, they were all dancing with each other, laughing, and having a great time.

The sun had long since dipped below the horizon when Anna announced they had to leave. "I feel bad leaving Kiley with Milo's mom for too long, even though she's super sweet about it. She swears Kiley will grow out of her hard stage. I hope she's right."

Milo blew out a weary breath as he stood. "Yeah, let's hope

we get a break before the teenage years hit. Congratulations to Noelle and Kade. Thanks for a great evening, Zoe."

"And Asher," Zoe added. "I couldn't have done it without him."

Kade arched his brow. "You two ever think about hooking up? You look good together. Maybe Jenkins is really cupid in disguise."

The air tightened, and Zoe refused to look at Asher.

"Kade," Noelle whispered in warning.

Asher broke the silence when he barked a laugh. "I hate to say this right before the two of you get married, but marital bliss can be a bitch if you pick the wrong person. I'm steering clear of that mess."

Zoe swallowed her hurt feelings and smiled as though his words didn't matter. "We're good friends, and that seems to work for us. Right, Asher?"

He winked at her. "That's right. I'm with you on that one."

Slowly, the couples departed, and the awkwardness returned when they were alone again. Zoe avoided his gaze by concentrating on cleaning up the rest of their things. Once again, Asher helped until they had everything finished.

"You headed upstairs?" he asked as they put away the last of the dishes.

The thought of being trapped in her bedroom with her ruthless thoughts stifled her. "Nah. I'm going to sit outside for a while. It's a nice night, and I'm feeling restless."

He agreed with a nod. "Yeah, it's hard to go from party to quiet so fast."

She snagged a beer from the fridge and headed for the door. "Don't wait up for me."

The serene night air surrounded her as she closed the door behind her and exhaled a sigh. She turned on soft music and inhaled deeply. Such a beautiful night. Such an adorable place that already felt like home. It might kill her if she was the one who had to leave.

It would be hard not to see Asher's haunting eyes every morning and every night. But if she had to move somewhere, like the dank basement apartment where she'd existed for years, she would wither away like a lonely flower left in an unwatered pot.

She was trapped in an impossible situation. Both outcomes would be a hard load to bear.

A warm breeze teased her hair, sending it dancing across her shoulders. Slowly, she walked to the table and ran her fingers over the wood. It was beautiful work.

With one hand, she shook it, impressed by how sturdy it was. There wasn't much about Asher Campbell that didn't impress her. He was as skilled with power tools as he was in the kitchen. And the good Lord knew she'd never forget the sight of him in his briefs.

She sighed as she slipped into a chair and leaned back, closing her eyes. A chorus of crickets sang with the music while her mind tumbled over Asher and his declaration of bachelorhood. She couldn't blame him. She knew how deeply Dana had hurt him.

If the universe would grant her a wish, she'd erase the years he'd spent with Dana from his mind. Or better yet, she'd transport them back in time and make sure he was hers long before Dana ever arrived on the scene.

18

sher couldn't stop looking. He'd gone upstairs to brush his teeth and had caught sight of Zoe through his bedroom window.

She looked so beautiful. So heartbreakingly lonely.

He wished he'd met her first, wished he'd loved her before anyone else. He should have acted instead of hesitating all those years ago. There was nothing worse than connecting with the right person at the wrong time.

Her blond curls cascaded over her bare shoulders, begging to be touched. She had her face tilted heavenward with her eyes closed. But he could easily conjure the depths of her engaging brown eyes. And her smile. The real one. Not the fake one she pasted on every so often as she had earlier that evening.

Something bothered her. No doubt. He wished he knew what it was so he might help her.

But she had a stubborn, closed side to her that was impenetrable if she wanted.

When she'd walked downstairs earlier, his heart had lit up like so many stars in the night sky. He'd used every bit of his resolve not to touch her, not kiss her like she needed to be kissed. If not by him, then by someone smarter, who hadn't been tainted by love.

Seeing her now breathed fire into him. He wanted to pull her into his arms, to give her a night she'd never forget. But the morning would come, and he didn't know if he could ever commit to a woman again. She deserved better than that. Better than him.

She wrapped her arms around her as though she might be chilled. Seconds later, she moved her fingertips across her bare arm as though a lover caressed her. Slowly, she trailed fingers up her shoulder as though savoring the feeling and then down the valley between her breasts.

He swallowed but couldn't dislodge the hard lump in his throat. She drew the backs of her fingers over her breast before they settled on her arm again, leaving his groan echoing through the quiet bedroom. *What the hell was wrong with him? Why couldn't he just love her?* She hadn't pushed him away when he'd kissed her before, and he didn't think she would now.

More than that, she wasn't Dana. He couldn't judge everyone by his ex's actions.

He couldn't look away. Not while Zoe was still within view. She'd bewitched him with her laugh, with her smile. Walking away would be like giving up oxygen.

She stroked her neck, her cheek, and he knew without a doubt she imagined a lover's touch. Was he in her mind? Or someone else?

When she traced her lips with the pad of her thumb, he knew he had to stop her. He couldn't look away, but he couldn't leave her out there like that alone. Maybe some conversation would distract them both.

He took the stairs two at a time and hurried until he reached the door. Then he softly opened it, not wanting to startle her, and stepped outside. She didn't open her eyes as he approached, and he wondered if she'd heard him, or if she was too lost in her fantasy world.

When he stopped next to her, she lifted her lids, her gaze serious, mesmerizing.

Neither spoke, but the look in her eye told him everything he did and didn't want to know.

He'd thought he couldn't look away while he'd watched from above, but that was nothing compared to being in her presence. Her chest rose and fell. With his gaze, he followed the path her fingers had taken earlier. He wanted to be the one who touched her, the lover she'd imagined.

"Zoe," he whispered, and then cleared his throat. "Do you mind if I join you?"

"Of course not," she said as she straightened in her seat.

A deep, pulsing current circled between them, but he resisted its pull as he dragged a chair closer and sat. "I guess I'm too wound up to sleep, too."

She gave him a soft smile. "It's so nice out here tonight."

He sensed an edginess about her, as though the calm expression she showed on the outside clashed violently with what was within. "Perfect evening. Everyone had a good time."

"I think so, too," she said. "Milo was on a roll telling the story of how he and Anna met. Who would have ever expected the mob?"

Asher snorted. "Yeah. That's the most excitement this town has seen."

She slid her gaze to him. "We shouldn't have gone all these years without being friends. I'm sorry I let things come between us. Looking back, it all seems so silly."

His laugh echoed above the music. "If I would have manned up, we would have been friends."

"Funny the changes life brings." She turned her head toward the radio when the song switched. "Wow. I haven't heard that song in forever. I swear they played it twenty times a day our senior year. Do you remember it?"

"Oh yeah. I do." He gave a derisive chuckle. "And it's come back to haunt me."

She tilted her head in question. "How do you mean?"

He shook his head, cursing himself. "This was the theme song for prom that year."

Zoe nodded slowly. "That's right. I'd forgotten."

He held her gaze for several long seconds. "I don't know why I asked Emily instead of you. I still remember that day. When I walked up, I was coming to ask you, and then I couldn't do it. So I made it seem like I'd intended to ask her all along."

She shook her head and softly snorted. "You were such a chicken."

"I was. But I'm not now." He stood and held out a hand. "Let me make it up to you. Dance with me, Zoe."

She hesitated a moment, and then the smile returned to her face. She accepted his offering and stood.

His pulse increased several notches as he slid a hand behind her back, resting it above the curve of her ass. She shook her cascade of curls from her shoulders as she turned her face upward to meet his gaze.

He thought about withholding his next words, but he wanted to erase the sadness he knew burned in her heart. "I know I shouldn't say this, but I can't help it. You look so beautiful tonight, Zoe. This dress. Your hair."

A genuine smile crept across her lips. "Thank you."

He wound a strand of hair around his finger, empowered by

her response to him. "These curls are so sexy. Makes a guy want to—"

He stopped himself before he said too much.

She laughed. "Oh, really?"

"Well…" He shrugged and grinned, knowing she'd deciphered his meaning, anyway.

She pulled the strand from his fingers, searching his gaze. "You're going to kiss me again, aren't you?"

Her question caught him off-guard, and he realized that was exactly what he wanted to do. He searched for the determination to resist that had served him well earlier in the night, but it was as long gone as Jenkins, and he was left with a beautiful woman.

"Don't bother trying to think your way out of this one," she said with a laugh.

Her breasts brushed his chest as they danced, chasing away his coherent thoughts. "Fine. I'll admit that I've thought about kissing you all night."

"Oh…"

Her breathless response charmed the hell out of him. "You asked."

She looked at him without fully tilting her face, as though she couldn't gaze at him directly. "All night?"

God knew he shouldn't have stepped outside the safety of the house, but it was too late for him now. "All night."

They were inches apart, and currents of attraction jumped between them like a thousand lightning strikes. She put a hand on his chest and seduced him with the sweet curve of her pink lips.

"Zoe," he said again, knowing he traveled a dangerous road.

She shook her head and put her fingers on his lips. "Don't tell me no, Asher. Please don't say no." She slid a hand behind his neck and drew his head toward hers.

Her words shot him full of need, and he couldn't move. Couldn't deny her.

She stood on tiptoe and claimed him with her kiss.

Soft. Powerful. Sweeter and more addictive than anything he'd experienced in his life. God help him, he couldn't stop. Not now.

He needed to own her. To possess her.

Nothing less would satisfy the raging animal inside him. Without breaking their kiss, he pulled her tighter against him.

A soft gasp escaped her lovely mouth, and she wrapped her arms around him. Tempting curves teased his body, and he rubbed his hands down her sides and over her ass.

She leaned into him, hardening his desire, drawing him past his breaking point.

"Zoe," he said between kisses. "I can't make you any promises beyond tonight, and I don't want to hurt you."

"I don't care about tomorrow." She pulled his head toward hers and kissed him with a thirst that drove him crazy with need. "I want this now."

How many times had he envisioned taking her in his arms? Pictured what she might look like as he undressed her and feasted on her body both visually and physically.

Nothing he'd imagined was anything like this.

With his breaths coming fast, he leaned away from her, needing to see the emotion on her face, in her eyes.

Her breasts heaved as she drew oxygen deep into her lungs. He traced the path she'd blazed earlier when he'd watched from his window, testing the softness of her arms, her shoulders.

With deliberate slowness, he buried his fingers in her luxurious mane and kissed her deeply.

Her soft cry of need rumbled through his chest like an earthquake, begging him to go faster. She stared at him, her eyes darker than the night. He held her gaze as he slid one strap from her shoulder.

He hadn't bared much of her skin, but he took a moment to savor what he'd uncovered. Her skin was the softest velvet as he kissed along her shoulder. A sexy floral scent surrounded her, and he inhaled deeply, burning the smell into his memory forever.

He savored every inch of sweetness as he plied kisses up her neck and ended in the soft hollow beneath her ear. She nuzzled against him.

"I've wanted you for so long," he whispered.

"How long?" she asked softly.

The truth of it anchored deep inside him. "For as long as I can remember."

She slid her hands up his chest, molding her fingers to the curve of his pecs. "Then there's no reason either of us should wait any longer."

The last of his resistance deserted him. "Maybe you're right. Maybe I worry too much. Maybe this is how things were always meant to be."

She placed two fingers on his lips. "Shh... You don't need to make promises. I only want tonight, Asher. Just tonight." She lifted her hand behind her back and slid down the zipper on her dress, moving away from him in the slightest as she did.

His breath jammed in his throat as his heart went ballistic. She slipped the dress from her shoulders, tugged it down her body, and let it puddle at her feet. Her breasts swelled from a black lace bra. Matching panties barely covered what he craved the most. So much lovely skin he ached to touch and kiss. And all of this was within his reach.

Ecstasy stood in front of him in the prettiest package he'd ever seen. "God, you're beautiful. I always knew you would be."

She was his if he wanted, and what sane man would turn her away? She wanted nothing more than a night with him.

Need radiated from her body, calling to him like a sweet siren's song, leaving him hazy with lust. "Can you tell me no now?" she whispered.

Doing so would be the death of him. "Damn, girl."

He closed the space between them, filling his hands with her soft flesh. The moment he'd always dreamed of became a reality.

19

Zoe gasped when he finally claimed her. The delicious feel of his hands on her skin, searching and caressing, nearly sent her over the edge. His touch, his kisses, carried a powerful urgency, as though she'd woken a sleeping giant.

Asher wouldn't leave her wanting this time.

He fisted his hands in her hair and tugged, forcing her to arch her throat. "When I watched you tonight, I imagined doing this."

He trailed a finger down her neck to the valley between her breasts and then followed with slow, deliberate kisses. Each time his lips met her skin, a new shiver erupted, sending fiery energy to her most sensitive areas.

She'd only been with two men in her life and neither experience carried half the intensity of what she now felt. "Asher," she whispered, overwhelmed by each sensation.

He paused, a sensual fire burning in his eyes. "Do you want me to stop?"

"No," she said breathlessly. *Never.*

He held her gaze as he spanned his large hands over each side of her waist, and then slowly he drew his fingers upward until they reached the undersides of her breasts. Thumbs crested her mounds, tightening her nipples into highly sensitive points.

She released a shaky breath, only to suck it in again as his hands followed the band of her bra to her back. Her skin tingled and burned where he touched her. She couldn't focus on anything else. Her bra tightened against her as he slipped fingers beneath it, and then, like an unexpected rush of cool wind, he set her free.

He drew the lacy garment away and dropped it on the nearby table.

"Oh, Zoe." His intake of breath stole hers. "You're so, so beautiful."

She trailed her fingers over his strong shoulders as he cupped her breasts, her gasp echoing into the night when he sucked a nipple into his mouth.

"Dear God," she whispered. He circled the tight bud with his tongue and then drew her deep into his mouth again, tightening everything inside into a delicious ball of need.

She slid her fingers into his hair, held him as he made sweet love to her breasts. Every inch of her was on fire, and she needed more.

With insistent fingers, she tugged his shirt upward, finding and delighting in the hard muscles beneath. "I need your skin against mine."

He paused his tender assault long enough to pull the shirt over his head before he cast it aside. Then he tugged her against his bare chest and held her tightly. She closed her eyes and reveled in the feel of him next to her.

"Jesus, you feel good," he whispered against her ear.

"You, too." He held her like she belonged to him, and she wondered if she'd ever be happy until she did.

She lifted her gaze, placing her palm against his cheek. "Don't make me wait any longer, Asher."

A deep rumble of desire echoed from his chest. He lifted her, earning a gasp of surprise, and carried her toward the lawn.

"Outside?" she asked as he laid her on the cool blanket of grass.

"Here. Now."

She wasn't about to argue.

He removed his pants and briefs, and stood before her like a god capable of owning her heart and her world. She stared breathlessly as he fished his wallet from his jeans and retrieved a condom. She couldn't stop tracing the powerful lines of his legs, shivering when she considered what he was about to do with the hard cock jutting from him.

Breaths were impossible as he joined her on the grass and knelt near her feet. He didn't ask, but slipped his fingers beneath her panties and tugged them off. But instead of joining her, he settled with his shoulders next to her thighs.

Her nerves flamed when she realized his intent. She caught his head with her hands. "Asher?"

He drew a finger between her folds, the feel of him like hot lightning on her skin. "You wanted me to love you, and that's exactly what I'm going to do."

"Asher," she said again as her control slipped.

He dipped his head, his tongue tracing the path his finger had taken, coaxing a moan of pleasure from her lips as a tremor rocked her body.

He laughed softly and repeated the tender assault, drawing her into an extraordinary place of indescribable bliss.

When he'd brought her to a crescendo and left sweet pleasure rolling through her, he moved up her body and claimed a breast, drawing a nipple into his heated mouth.

"Oh, God, Asher. I never..."

He captured her face between his hands and kissed her hard. "Maybe it's wrong to want this," he said after ending their kiss. "But I intend to ruin you for any lesser man. This is what you deserve, Zoe. Never settle for anything less."

Emotion clogged her throat as he possessed her mouth again. She wanted to ask exactly what he'd meant, but he quickly stole all rational thoughts as he slipped inside her.

She gasped and arched, wanting to take as much of him as she could. She needed to feel him in the depths of her soul.

He withdrew and filled her again until nothing existed but him. Nothing mattered but right here, right now, and the feel of him inside her.

She clung to him as he made love to her again, bringing her to another orgasm before he finally claimed one for himself. She held him tight as he trembled over her, and deep breaths escaped them both.

A soft summer breeze cooled her heated body as he rolled and pulled her next to him. She lifted a leg and snuggled it between his thighs, molding against him as much as she could. His heart thundered beneath her cheek, and she ran a hand over his chest, needing to feel more of him.

Neither of them said a word for a long time.

Zoe didn't care. She was content to lie in his arms, listening to the crickets and gazing at the moon as it crested the hills.

"You're cold," he finally said, rubbing his hand over the arm resting on his chest.

"A little." But she didn't want to do anything that would jeopardize this moment.

"Let's go inside." His voice rumbled beneath her ear.

She lifted her head. "Will you stay with me tonight?"

He nodded slowly, thoughtfully.

They gathered their clothes and soon snuggled between the sheets on her bed. She worried they weren't talking, but he claimed her mouth with another heated kiss. It chased away her apprehension, replacing it with more exquisite sensations.

He'd wanted to ruin her for other men. And he had.

No one could ever make her feel the way she did that night.

20

Zoe woke slowly. As flashes from the previous night became fully fleshed memories, a smile crept across her face. She and Asher had made sweet love until deep into the star-soaked night.

Aching thighs and bruised lips provided further proof she hadn't dreamed her incredible night with Asher. He'd been so much more than she ever could have thought possible. He hadn't just made love to her; he'd made her feel loved, cherished even. She hadn't been fortunate to have experienced that before, but she had now, and it was the best thing ever.

She rolled in the sheets, looking forward to another round, or at least morning snuggles with Asher.

But the opposite side of the bed was empty.

She sat up and glanced at his pillow, not comforted by the indentation. As seconds passed, unwelcome worry slithered through her. That Asher wasn't with her meant nothing. Things between them were fine. She didn't need to fret.

She repeated those thoughts as she searched for the robe she rarely wore. Once bundled inside the cotton garment, she stepped into the hall. His bedroom door was open, so she hurried down the stairs into the kitchen.

Zoe found Asher fully dressed in a t-shirt, jeans and boots, sitting at the kitchen table with a cup of coffee, lines of concern marring his expression. He glanced up when she walked into the room.

"Good morning," she said, her voice full of hesitation.

He stood, walked to her, and gave her a kiss on the cheek. "Morning."

Dredges of relief gurgled inside her, although an unmistakable awkwardness filled the air. "I was worried when you weren't there when I woke up."

"What can I say? I'm an early riser." He gave her the briefest of smiles. "I'm headed out. Got a lot to do today."

She glanced at the clock. The hands hadn't quite reached eight a.m. "On a Sunday?"

"I'm helping a buddy." He took his keys from the hook on the wall and started to walk away.

She couldn't do this, couldn't spend the day wondering if things were okay. "Wait, Asher. What's wrong?"

"Nothing's wrong, Zoe. Don't make more out of it than what it is." He backed another step away from her. "I told you I couldn't give you anything beyond last night, and you said that was okay. You know I'm not ready for a serious relationship."

She also wasn't ready for the icy wall he'd erected around himself.

He was right, though. He'd warned her. She swallowed her shame. "I wasn't asking for anything more. But I need to know things are okay between us."

Fear shimmered in his eyes. "Why wouldn't they be? We're friends. Good friends, right?"

She forced a smile past her aching heart. "Right. Friends."

"Good. I'll see you later tonight." He turned and left without a backward glance.

As the sound of his truck tires on the gravel faded away, she collapsed into the chair he'd vacated. She'd gotten what she'd wanted. A night in his arms. He'd told her he couldn't offer her anything more, and she'd agreed.

Funny how midnight promises burned like hell in the daylight.

———

Asher strode inside Sparrow's Bar and Grill, with Seth by his side. His friend lifted his chin. "Get us a table, and I'll be right back."

As Seth headed toward the bathrooms, Asher strode through the cool, dim bar toward the pool tables in the rear. He picked a table and dropped into a seat.

A love song played over the sound system, bringing Zoe to the forefront of his thoughts. Again. Like he'd been able to think of anything but her.

He had avoided any serious conversations with her all week. Long hours on the job kept him busy until dark sent him home. By then, she was occupied with accounting work or had sequestered herself in her bedroom. She seemed as eager to avoid the obvious as he did.

He knew before he'd laid hands on her it would be a mistake, but he'd allowed himself to get caught up in the moment, entranced by the moonlight and a beautiful woman.

Didn't mean it was okay. He'd hurt her. He could see it every time he caught one of her brief gazes, and he loathed himself for it.

Problem was, he didn't know how to make things better.

When he thought about what life might be like if he let her in, his heart clenched and curled into a ball like an abused dog.

Becky, the bartender, approached. The friendly blonde didn't show as much cleavage as she had before she'd married, but she was still a terrible flirt. "The usual burger and soda, handsome? Seth want one, too?"

It was only lunchtime, and he still had a long day ahead of him. Already he was exhausted. Maybe food would help. "That'd be great, Becky."

"You doing okay?" she asked, instead of walking away.

For once, he wished she'd skip the small talk and fetch his lunch instead. "I'm good."

"Don't lie to me. I can see it in your eyes. Working too many hours, or is it problems at home?"

He knew she referred to Zoe. It seemed no matter how little he talked about his personal life, everyone in town had the full details any way. "Just some long ass days."

"I understand. Your business is booming. It's a lot of work, but I'm happy for you and Seth."

He dipped his chin in gratitude. "Thanks."

She paused a moment as though she had more to say, but then turned with a sigh and walked away. He was grateful for the reprieve.

Seth joined him a few moments later. "You order?"

"Yeah, for both of us."

"Good. I'm starving."

Becky returned with their drinks, and Seth downed half his soda immediately. When she returned a bit later and set their hamburgers before them, Asher's stomach turned, leaving a churning feeling inside. He felt similar to his younger days, when he'd stayed out too late the night before, partying with the boys.

He wished he could call it a day, but that wasn't happening, and he needed to talk, needed to spill his guts to someone. He took a long drink of soda and focused on his friend. "Gotta tell you something."

"Shoot," Seth said seconds before making a serious dent in his burger.

Asher eyed him with a serious look. "I did something I shouldn't have." Just mentioning it knotted him up inside.

Any joviality remaining on Seth's face disappeared. "You didn't. *Shit.* You slept with her."

"Dammit. How did you know?"

"Because you've been walking around like the apocalypse hit ever since the party. Neither of you could keep your eyes off each other then, and it was bound to happen. She's a beautiful woman, and you haven't had sex in, God, what is it? Over a year now? It was only a matter of time before you caved."

"Shit," Asher said under his breath. He lifted his burger and took a huge bite. If his mouth was full, he couldn't say anything more.

"Now what?" Seth asked.

Asher shook his head as he finished chewing. "Hell if I know. She's not happy. I'm not either."

"Problems satisfying her?" Seth asked with a straight face.

That certainly hadn't been their problem. "Hell. She's never had it so good."

"Hey," Seth said in a defensive tone. "It happens."

"Is it happening to you?" Asher shot back.

"Hell, no." He wasn't happy with the insinuation. Neither was Asher. "I know how to keep my woman happy," Seth said.

"Same here." Except Zoe wasn't his woman. "Now that we've discovered neither of us has an issue, can we talk about the real problem?"

Seth opened his hands, palms up. "Whenever you're ready, man."

Asher mentally cursed. "I slept with her, and now we're barely talking. I warned her I wasn't interested in anything serious, and she agreed. But she either lied or changed her mind."

He tilted his head in dismay. "Yep. That's a problem. Why don't you talk to her?"

Asher thought for a moment. "I don't know what the hell to say."

"Tell her how you're feeling. It works for me."

He dropped his forehead into his palm. "I did tell her. I explained I wasn't ready for a commitment and that we're good friends. Friends with benefits, I suppose. Or at least a one-time benefit."

"So you screwed her, and now you won't talk to her. I told you not to go down that road." Seth snorted like Asher was an idiot for not figuring that out for himself. "No wonder she doesn't want anything to do with you."

He agreed on the idiot part. "What do I do? I want things to go back to the way they were before. We had fun. We'd laugh and talk. Sex messed up everything."

Seth pointed a ketchup-tipped French fry in his direction. "Well, now that you've done the deed, you might as well move forward. I say you gotta stop being scared."

"I'm not." No way in hell. Except... "Okay, maybe I am. I like Zoe. I always have, but when I think of trying to make a life again with someone..." He shook his head instead of finishing his sentence.

His friend eyed him with a sharp look. "I'm not a shrink or anything, but my best advice is to face your fears. Zoe's a nice lady like you said. You need to date again. Why not with her? You could do much worse."

That wasn't the answer he'd come looking for. "I need more time."

"Dude," Seth continued. "It's been a year. If you hadn't have slept with her already, I'd say you could go another couple of months. But you've done the deed. You might as well get back on the proverbial horse and see where it leads. It could be a hell of a ride."

Asher scoffed. "Aren't you the philosopher these days?"

"What are you afraid of?" Seth pinned him with a stare. "Don't answer. I already know. But do you? Do you see how you're hiding from life? Trust me. I've been there. If you don't start living, soon years will have gone by. Years you can't get back. Years that you're still allowing your ex to ruin because you're afraid to move on. You don't have to move fast, but maybe it's time to take a chance. A small chance."

Seth was right. He'd given Dana far too much of his life as it was. All for nothing. "So, it's that easy, then? Just pretend my past didn't happen and jump in head first?"

He shrugged. "What do you have to lose?"

"Besides my patched up heart? Nothing."

Seth lifted his soda in a toast. "Exactly."

Maybe it *was* time he manned up. He hadn't stepped up the first go round with Zoe and look where that had gotten him. "If I come out on the wrong end of this, swear to be my full-time drinking buddy for at least a month."

"Shit." Seth laughed and shook his head. "Just do it already."

———

Asher knocked off early that day. He'd put in a good forty hours that week already, and it was only Wednesday. He could afford a few hours to put the other side of his life back on track.

It was time he owned his shit.

He pulled into the parking lot of Andersen's Grocery before

he headed home. The store didn't have much in the way of fresh flowers, but at least they had some.

He brushed what dirt and dust he could off him and his clothes before he entered. Maybe he'd grab a pie or something from the bakery, too.

"Hey, Jeanine," Asher said as he entered and caught the store clerk's reply. He made a beeline straight for the flowers and stopped as he stared at the bouquets of different colored roses and others with colorful daisies.

"Shit." Which would be best? He was hesitant to go for the roses because he knew different colors had different meanings, but he'd be damned if he could remember which was which. He didn't want something that pledged eternal love, but if he gave her some that signified only friendship, he was sure to be screwed, too.

"Well, hello, Asher."

He turned at the sound of his name and found the worst gossiper in town standing a few feet behind him with a smile on her weathered face. "Afternoon, Earlene."

"Afternoon to you, too." She glanced down at the bouquets in front of them. "Picking flowers for someone special?"

He wasn't about to spill anything. "For my aunt. It's her birthday. Can you tell me which color of roses means what?"

"For her, I'd probably go with the peach or pink." She pointed toward a suitable bouquet. "I'm glad to hear you're not going for the red ones."

He didn't want to bite her bait, but couldn't resist. "Why not?" Out of all the colors, he liked the red ones best.

A sly smile stretched the wrinkles from her lips. "Love. A single red rose means I love you. If you'd picked those, I'd be worried about you."

A hefty dose of dread spilled over him. "Why would you be

afraid if I was in love?" Again, he didn't want to ask, but he couldn't stand the wondering.

She gave him a motherly pat on the arm. "Just hoping it wasn't that Zoe Cassidy that you were buying them for. I've heard that you're living together, but you need to be careful where she's concerned."

He was about ready to tell off the meddling old woman, but he'd hear her out first. "And why's that?"

Pleasure sparked in the old woman's eyes. "She's planning on lawyering-up, if she hasn't already. She's going to make sure she gets the Jenkins house, not you."

Tightness overtook his chest. Unfortunately, more often than not, she was right. "How do you know this?"

"Overheard her and Noelle Parker, soon-to-be Collier, talking at Rumors. If you haven't retained an attorney, I'd suggest that you do, too. It's certain to be a great pissing contest between the two of you when they never find Jenkins who ran off with all your money, but I like a fair fight, don't you?"

Shit. He withheld any expression of emotion. "Thanks for the tip. I'll look into things." Then he walked away with no flowers.

21

Zoe set her alarm twenty minutes earlier than usual. The chill between her and Asher had become nearly palpable during the past few days, and she hoped to catch him that morning before he headed off to work. Each day, he seemed to leave right before she woke, and he never came home before ten at night.

At first, she'd thought he'd increased the number of hours he worked in a day to capitalize on sunlight. But then he'd popped in at Rumors with Seth early yesterday, and Noelle reported he'd acted just fine. He hadn't said much to her, but she'd said it was obvious they were finished with work for the day, and yet, he still hadn't come home until after Zoe had gone to bed.

She'd come to the undeniable conclusion he was avoiding her.

She couldn't pretend that knowledge didn't hurt. Their night together had been amazing, but it had ruined everything between them. She couldn't begin to understand why. They'd meshed like honey and butter on warm bread. Until the next morning.

But enough was enough. Friends talked about things and didn't let problems fester. If he wouldn't start the conversation, she would.

She opened her bedroom door and heard him in the kitchen. After a quick stop in the bathroom, she headed downstairs, only to hear him closing the front door behind him. She raced out onto the porch, but his glowing taillights and dust were all that greeted her in the early morning light.

"Dammit," she yelled. She returned inside and slammed the door.

She knew he regretted their night together, but he couldn't hide behind his work forever. They needed to talk, to iron things out.

She wanted to love him, but if that was out of the question, then she'd resort to liking him until he'd fully healed from his failed marriage. She could wait.

What she couldn't tolerate was them reverting to their previous unbearable relationship. She wanted him in her life. No, after the way he'd loved her, she *needed* him in her life. She'd witnessed the raw, uninhibited side of him and his true heart, and she couldn't go back to pretending she hadn't. She couldn't let a love like that go without a fight.

If he couldn't give her the time of day, she'd go to the construction site after work.

———

Because of her early alarm, Zoe arrived at work ten minutes ahead of schedule. She said her normal hello to Mallory, who manned the front desk at city hall and headed down to unlock her office. She hadn't been in her seat two minutes when Mallory appeared at the door.

"Zoe?" The receptionist had the best legs in town, and Zoe envied her every time she wore a skirt.

"What's up, Mallory?" The dismay etched on her face warned of bad news. "Did something happen?"

The woman hesitated a moment and then strode forward and dropped a tri-folded paper on her desk. "I'm sorry."

Zoe frowned as she picked up the paper and smoothed it out in front of her. She quickly scanned the contents of what looked to be the first page of a legal document. Her name appeared, along with Asher's.

She lifted her gaze to Mallory. "What's this?"

"Mariam over at the Pinecone Courthouse mentioned to me she'd seen a document come across her desk, and she'd asked if you and Asher still lived together. I asked why. She explained Asher's lawyer had filed paperwork to have a judge determine ownership of your house. But it seemed so unlikely to me because I know you and Asher have been getting along great. In fact, people are betting on which month he'll ask you to marry him."

The speed and delivery method with which Mallory imparted information left her head spinning. "They are?"

"That doesn't matter." She waved her hand as though to dismiss her last comment. "What matters is I didn't believe her, so I asked for proof. She faxed the first page of that document."

Mallory paused and focused a solemn gaze on her. "Zoe, Asher's out to prove the house is his and force you to move out."

Her friend's declaration would have knocked her off her feet if she'd been standing. "He wouldn't," she whispered.

They'd agreed to remain friends regardless of what happened, hadn't they? She couldn't for a minute believe he'd hurt her this way just because he regretted having sex with her.

Mallory gave her a sad smile. "It's there in black and white. I'm certain they'll give you notice in the next couple of days, if not today." She dropped her gaze and then looked at Zoe again. "I'm so sorry to give you this news. Obviously, I've shocked you. I could have sat on it, but I felt you deserved a heads-up and to hear it from someone who cares about you as opposed to the gossip train."

Zoe shook her head as she held up a shaking hand. "No, no. It's all right. I'm glad you told me."

She shifted her gaze to the insulting, hurtful document in front of her and read it again. In a corner of her mind, she heard Mallory excuse herself, but Zoe couldn't ignore her thoughts long enough to answer.

How could he? The question repeated in her mind like a broken recording. Had he planned this all along? Could she really have been so naïve?

Anger quickly replaced confusion and pain.

He would not get away with this.

She left a sticky note on the outside of her office promising to return in an hour. She briefly said goodbye to Mallory and stepped into the harsh morning light.

It took her all of five minutes to reach the growing subdivision. The house she'd visited the first time appeared to be complete, and they'd poured two new foundations as the basis for several others.

She parked behind Asher's truck and noted another truck sitting down the street. She prayed Seth wouldn't be inside with Asher. But even if he was, she intended to have it out with her housemate once and for all.

She stepped inside the unfinished home and caught the unmistakable scent of sawdust. A moment later, the sound of a saw working echoed off the bare wood. She followed the noise and made her way over the discarded housing material toward the back of the house.

Asher caught sight of her the second she stepped into the

room. He stopped the saw and slowly the ringing died away. His gaze was hard, brutal, and she found no sign of the man she'd fallen for.

"Bastard." Tears stung her eyes and fell down her cheeks. "I should have trusted my original instincts and stayed far away from you."

Anger flared in his eyes like a wildfire that had jumped the fire line. "What the hell did you expect me to do, Zoe? Take it in the ass and not fight back? I've already made the mistake of trusting one woman, and I don't intend to do that again."

God, he was hard. Cruel even. "So, is this a strike first kind of thing? Is that it? Did you lie when you promised we'd always be friends? Was that a way to get me to lower my guard?" Her heart thumped hard enough in her chest to make her nauseous.

He narrowed his eyes in disgust. "Give it up, Zoe. I know what you did. Don't act like I'm the bad guy. You're the one who lied."

"I didn't lie." Her voice hit a tone that left her uncomfortable. "I've been nothing but nice to you since we patched things up between us. God, I even let you take me to bed."

He pointed a sharp finger at her. "*You're* the one who seduced me."

Acid tears burned her cheeks as she slowly shook her head. She couldn't believe he'd toss that in her face. "No," she whispered. "I loved you."

She turned and walked away.

She hadn't made it far before he grabbed her shoulder and turned her around. "I'm not going to let you make me out to be the bad guy. You're the one who destroyed this. Just when I thought maybe I could trust again, you went behind my back and retained a lawyer."

She swallowed past the thick lump in her throat. "I didn't,

Asher. I don't know where you get your information from, but you're wrong. Dead wrong."

He clamped his mouth shut, but continued to glare.

She placed a hand against her shredded heart, willing it to continue to beat. "Just because one woman betrayed you doesn't mean all women will. You have a real problem, Asher Campbell, and you need to get over yourself."

She caught a second breath. "If you want to wallow in the past and stay stuck there forever, be my guest. I'm done with you, done with everything. I'd hoped in time you could heal enough to let me in, but I doubt you're capable. You're a broken, pathetic excuse for a man."

Her verbal arrow had the desired effect. Anguish exploded in his eyes, but she quickly erected a shield to keep her heart from succumbing to guilt.

She turned and strode from the room, telling herself she'd done the right thing. Her thoughts full of images and conversations from all the times he'd pushed her away fortified her. She'd been such a fool to think they might have had a future. She'd been the only one who'd made efforts in that direction while he'd done nothing but erect roadblocks.

She stumbled down the last step, but righted herself before she fell.

An image of his ex-wife doing the same increased the sick feeling in her stomach. How had she'd become entangled in such a mess?

Maybe some people were too broken to be fixed. One thing was for sure. She didn't intend to stick around and become one of them.

22

Zoe woke the next morning, stiff from sleeping on Noelle's couch. She hadn't returned to work the previous day and had stopped by her house only long enough to gather a few items. She needed time and distance away from the ugliness that now pervaded her once beloved home.

Asher could have the place. It would no longer provide the solace it once had for her. In fact, one of the first things on her list that morning would be to stop by her previous residence to see if there was a chance the tiny, dark apartment was still available. The basement might be oppressive, but at least she hadn't experienced such pain and disappointment there.

She opted to skip breakfast, since her stomach couldn't tolerate food. Instead, she made her excuses to Noelle and slipped into her car.

Surreptitiously, she drove past their house, glancing to be sure Asher had already left for work. When she didn't find his truck in the drive, she circled around and parked in front.

Their house.

What a joke. Her house? His house? Jenkins' house? Who

the hell knew who owed the damned place? But it definitely wasn't *their* house.

Leaving might cost her every cent she'd saved for years, but she couldn't put a price on her sanity.

She unlocked the door and stepped inside. The shock of seeing so many items missing stopped her in her tracks. The TV. The couch. The painting of a pack of wolves Asher had hung on the wall.

For a second, she wondered if someone had robbed them. But deep down, she knew. *She knew.*

Asher had packed up and left her.

The hollowness echoing through her was deeper than a bottomless well. He was gone. And she'd been far too easy to leave.

She hurried up the stairs to his bedroom, hoping somehow she was wrong. But when she slowly opened the door, the inside was empty. Barren, like her heart.

Her better senses tried to convince her that his leaving was for the best. But her heart resounded with the hollowness of another failed chance at love.

She sank to the floor, no longer knowing whether she should pack up or stick around. With Asher gone, she had no reason to hurry and leave. But she wasn't sure if she could stay in the lonely old house without him.

***

Asher sat the last moving box on the top of a stack inside the musty, dimly lit enclosure and focused on Milo. "Thanks for letting me dump all my stuff back in your barn."

"Not a problem. Are you sure you don't want to reclaim our spare room, too?"

He shook his head. "Nah. I can camp out at Jeremy's until I figure out what I'm doing next."

"Quieter there?" Milo gave him a conspiratorial grin, and Asher chuckled.

"Kiley's a doll," Asher said, instead of confessing.

Milo laughed. "A very loud doll."

Asher gave him a half nod and then sat on one stack of boxes. Too many things weighed heavily on his mind, and he couldn't bear any of them any longer. "Dana finally paid me for the equity in the house." He glanced up to catch Milo's solemn nod.

"That's good." He seemed hopeful. "Is that why you moved out? Because you have the money for something else?"

His nod turned to a shake of his head. "I moved out to give Zoe some space. She doesn't need an asshole like me hanging around."

Milo frowned. "What the hell kind of talk is that? I thought the two of you were getting along."

"I'm too screwed up to get along with anyone." He raked his fingers through his hair. "Dana messed me up good, and I'm too broken to be fixed."

Milo scoffed. "I ought to punch you in the mouth for that. Do you hear yourself?"

Asher stood and faced him eye-to-eye. "When you've walked in my shoes, then you can judge me. Imagine learning Anna had been with another man. In your bed. Tell me that wouldn't mess you up and break something deep inside you."

Milo blinked. "No, it would. But think about it, Asher. How long are you going to let her continue to keep breaking you? You're not broke, you're stuck. When are you going to decide you've given enough to the woman who didn't appreciate you and start focusing on one that will?"

Milo might as well have punched him, since his words hit

harder than a fist to the jaw. "Yeah, okay. I get it. At least my head gets it, but my heart is still stuck in that place. I've tried to wrench it out, but every time I take a step forward, I end up stumbling and then taking two steps back. It feels like I'm spinning my damn wheels."

"Then I guess you give the vehicle more gas. Keep pushing forward. Keep fighting. Keep trying to move on with your life. One day it will work." Milo shook his head. "The only other option isn't acceptable. Maybe you should give Zoe a chance."

Asher sank to the boxes. "I screwed that up as well." He filled Milo in on the details of what he'd done to Zoe, and then how he'd learned the truth that she hadn't betrayed him after all.

Milo shook his head. "That's rough, man. The way I see it is you have two choices. If you think you might have a shot at happiness with Zoe, try to mend things. If not, move on to the next thing in life. But don't look back. Don't ever look back."

Asher silently agreed with a nod. "I'm going to get going. Need to get to bed so I can get up early." Even saying that, he knew thoughts of Zoe would chase away any chance of sleep that night and for many more to come.

23

Zoe returned home after a long day at work and frowned at the familiar, older Cadillac parked outside her house. No one was inside the car and Betty Johnson, the local realtor, wasn't in sight, either. Zoe parked her car, slipped her cell phone out of her purse, and quickly dialed Noelle's number.

"Hey," Zoe said when she answered. "Betty still drives that old Cadillac, right?"

At Noelle's confirmation, she continued. "For whatever reason, her car is here, but she isn't. Something doesn't feel right."

"That's odd," Noelle replied. "Want me to call her husband?"

"Maybe..." Zoe said as she surveyed her surroundings. "Is it okay if I keep you on the phone while I look around first?"

"Absolutely."

Heightened awareness sent caution skittering up her back like a squirrel running up a tree. Zoe climbed the porch stairs and checked the front door. Locked. She slipped her key in the hole and turned the knob.

"Hello?" she called out, but didn't receive a response. "It doesn't look like anyone's here," she said to Noelle.

"Maybe her car broke down, and she found a ride into town?" Noelle offered.

"Yeah, maybe." Zoe walked through the house and into the kitchen to peek out the window. No one was there, either.

Zoe returned to the front and was about to climb the staircase when the front door burst open, leaving her gasping in surprise. She'd gathered lungs full of air, but the scream died in her throat when Bob Jenkins appeared like a ghost from the past.

The lines in his weathered face had deepened, and he appeared much thinner. He scanned the room, looking confused, took one look at her, and frowned.

"Bob," she heard a woman call out from behind him, and then Betty came into view.

"Oh, God. There you are, Zoe. Bob showed up at my business not long ago, and I knew you'd want to see him right away."

"What are you doing in my house?" he asked with a confused look. "Where's my goddamn stuff?"

"I've got to go," Zoe told Noelle. "Bob Jenkins just showed up."

"*What?*"

"Yeah, with Betty. Fill you in later." Zoe ended the call.

Betty tapped her temple, warning that Bob might not be in his right mind. "I probably should have called the police, but I didn't want to cause a ruckus unless I needed to."

Jenkins glanced over his shoulder. "Damn right you should have. I've been usurped by this thief," he declared.

Zoe widened her eyes in shock. "Mr. Jenkins, I'm Zoe Cassidy. Remember me? You sold your home to me a few months ago."

He frowned and seemed to fall into deep thought. A moment later, he shook his head vehemently. "No. I sold my house to Asher Campbell. Isn't that right, Betty?"

Betty gave him a kind smile. "Actually, I helped you with the sale to Zoe. But there were some complications. Zoe, do you think you have lemonade or something in the fridge for Mr. Jenkins? He should sit while we make a few phone calls."

Milo and Sheriff Reynolds arrived a mere fifteen minutes later, both offering her wide-eyed expressions when she let them into the house.

The sheriff was old enough to be her dad, but still quite handsome, with silver strands threading his dark hair. As always, he carried the air of authority that went with his title.

"He just showed up?" the sheriff asked in a low tone.

"He went to Betty's first, and she brought him here," Zoe answered quietly. "He seems very confused. Betty's distracting him in the kitchen right now. He thinks I've robbed him of his things and seems to be more agitated when he sees me. I get the impression he remembers some of what happened, but when he tries to recall out loud, he gets frustrated and angry with me."

Milo marched past her. "Let's talk to him. See what he has to say."

Zoe let Sheriff Reynolds pass, too, and then she followed behind, hoping to stay out of the old man's immediate view.

The sheriff approached the older man and stuck out a friendly hand. "Hey, Bob. How the hell are you?"

He glowered. "I'd be all right if I knew what happened to all my stuff. Zoe moved it out whilst I was gone and brought all her things in here. I'd like you to question her and help me get everything back. She probably ought to go to jail, too."

Zoe rolled her eyes. If anyone deserved incarceration, the

old man did. Except it was obvious he hadn't duped them on purpose.

Milo clapped him on the back before he took the seat next to him. "We'll look into that. First, though, I need to get more information from you. Would that be all right?"

Jenkins stared at Milo for a moment and then gave him a brief nod. "I 'spose so if it'll help me get my stuff back."

Milo offered a kind smile along with his gently probing words. "Bob, do you remember contacting Betty a while ago and telling her you wanted to sell your home?"

He seemed to consider the question as he scratched his scruffy gray beard. "I guess I do."

"That's right." Sheriff Reynolds nodded as he briefly met Zoe's gaze. "You wanted to sell it after Margaret died."

Grief the size of Texas struck his face, and he gripped the sheriff's arm with his bony fingers. "Margaret's dead?"

"Bob, Margaret has been dead now for three years. Remember her sudden stroke?" Milo said in a gentle tone. "We buried her in the cemetery and most of the town came."

Bob agreed, even though he had tears in his eyes. "I remember now. I put white roses on her grave. But it was too lonely here without her."

"That's right," Betty said, the tone of her voice encouraging him to continue. "So, you came to see me. You wanted to sell your house and use the money to travel."

Bob's expression brightened. "I did. I went all kinds of places, Vegas, and Colorado where they have that big canyon—"

He stopped abruptly. "But I didn't sell my place to that woman." He pointed an accusing finger at Zoe. "I let that nice boy Asher Campbell have it. Maybe she's stolen his stuff, too. You should arrest her."

Zoe stepped forward to defend herself, but halted when

Milo shook his head. She folded her arms and remained silent while animosity and frustration stewed inside her.

"Mr. Jenkins, do you have the money that Asher gave you for the house?" Milo prodded.

The old man scratched his chin again. "I think so. I must have left it at that bank in Vegas." He nodded firmly. "Yes, that's what I did."

"Do you remember which bank?" the sheriff asked.

"Uh...uh..." He leaned over and pulled out his wallet. Several fifty-dollar bills fell to the floor as he rifled through the contents, but he didn't seem to notice as he held out a stack of white receipts. "Do any of these tell you?"

Zoe eyed them, knowing what they held could make her day or send it spiraling like a plane out of fuel.

Sheriff Reynolds took the stack and began a slow process of opening each folded paper, reading it, and then moving it to another pile.

After several minutes of excruciating suspense, he halted. "Bank of Las Vegas. This appears to be a deposit slip in the amount of twenty thousand dollars."

"That would be correct," Jenkins said with a grin, revealing crooked, yellow teeth.

"That's what *I* paid for it," Zoe said in a hushed voice.

The sheriff continued his investigation of the contents of Mr. Jenkins' wallet. "What else do you have here? Looks like another deposit slip for ten thousand."

"No, that can't be right. It was twenty thousand," Jenkins offered, shaking his head.

Sheriff Reynolds held up two bank slips. "Yes, the twenty thousand is there, but also another ten thousand."

Zoe narrowed her gaze at the old man. Not only had he called her a liar and a thief, but he'd made her put down double what he'd asked from Asher.

The sheriff patted Jenkins on the shoulder. "Thanks for that information. It should help us sort things out."

"Good. You gonna put her in jail now?" Jenkins switched his gaze to her, looking like a mountain lion ready to nail his prey, and she wondered what she'd ever done to earn his animosity.

"Let's see what we find first. If she's guilty, we'll certainly take her in." Milo nodded reassuringly.

Sheriff Reynolds exited the kitchen, with his deputy walking close behind. Zoe followed. The sheriff handed the bank receipts to Milo. "Get on this. See what they can tell us. I'd like to know the balance of his account. We'll likely require a search warrant to get information, but I'd like that along with obtaining copies of checks he deposited. This will give us a better indication of who owns the home."

Zoe shouldn't have been listening to their private conversation, but she had a lot at stake here. "Milo? Sheriff?" she said, stepping forward. "What's going to happen now?"

Sheriff Reynolds shrugged. "Hard to say exactly at this point. We'll determine how much cash Jenkins spent. We should also be able to see who paid for the house first. I know a warranty deed and trust deed have been drawn up for you by Betty, but those may be negated depending on the date he sold to Asher." He gave her a commiserating smile. "As hard as it may be, you'll have to wait a bit longer."

She exhaled and nodded. "I understand. Call me as soon as you learn anything, okay?"

"You know we will," Milo offered. "Betty's talking to Jenkins now, convincing him to stay at the motel until we figure out what's happened, since none of his stuff is here. I'm going to ask one of his old friends to stay with him to keep him from wandering off. Then we'll have to see about finding a care facility for him that can help with his problems, since he has no known family to care for him."

Her empathy kicked in full force. "I'm sorry. That seems really awful for him." He was so lost and didn't know it.

Milo gave her a friendly pat on the shoulder. "Hang in there, Zoe. I'm headed to find Asher and fill him in on the news."

Despair rose inside her. She wanted to ask Milo about Asher, about how he'd been doing the past few days, but she couldn't bring herself to say anything. He'd killed whatever they might have had between them. "Okay. I'm sure he'll be relieved."

Twenty minutes later, the house was quiet again.

She glanced around at her little half-filled home as loneliness echoed from the bare walls. Their day of reckoning had finally come.

The state of her heart mimicked the house, and she realized it didn't matter if she or Asher was the true owner. He was broken inside, and she couldn't get past the thought that now she was as well.

24

Zoe sat on her front porch, watching as Noelle drove down the gravel lane toward her house. The sun drew closer to the horizon, casting a spectacular pink hue over the land. She urged her heart to open up enough to enjoy it.

During the past few weeks, she'd worked hard to achieve a smidgen of happiness in her life. Memories of Asher still haunted the place and her dreams, but she hoped eventually they'd fade. She'd focused on gratitude, and she'd been able to include ownership of the house on that list. Now she could add gorgeous sunsets to her inventory.

It turned out Asher had been the actual owner of the house, but he'd signed over his ownership for cash before she'd had a chance to fight against it. Her mortgage was already in effect, while his had been put on hold, making it much easier to cancel.

Still, she had her home. The same place she'd intended to make her haven all those months ago, and she was now determined to achieve that again.

They said people entered others' lives for a reason. She

couldn't fathom why Asher had come into hers. She'd already experienced loss and the unexplainable inability to elicit the love she needed from others. She hadn't needed that painful lesson again.

"Hey," Noelle called as she exited her car carrying a white paper sack.

Zoe knew what the bag contained and grinned. "Hi, there."

"What are you doing?" Noelle asked as she approached.

"Looking at this garden in front of the window, thinking I should plant tulips that will come up in the spring. Red. Maybe pink. Or maybe a crazy mix of all colors."

"Sounds pretty." She held out the bag. "I brought you some crack cocaine."

Zoe snorted, peeking inside to find two cinnamon rolls stacked in plastic containers. "The cops will get you for distribution one of these days."

Noelle smiled and sat next to Zoe. "I just wanted to make sure you're doing okay."

She forced the smile she'd used so often these days. "Of course I am. Why wouldn't I be?"

"Hmm..." Noelle said as she gazed out across the open fields. "Kade saw Asher today."

Zoe remained silent.

Her friend caught her with a sideways glance. "He's as miserable as you are, you know?"

She huffed softly. "You don't have to make me feel better. He's where he wants to be." Alone. Like she was.

"You know how guys are. They never know what's best for them until they don't have it."

She snorted. Fat lot of good that did her.

Noelle gently elbowed her. "I think you need to give him another chance."

Her tender heart forced her to stiffen. "Like I said, he's

where he wants to be." Not to mention she wouldn't survive if he turned her down again. She'd barely gotten her feet under her.

"Okay...well..." Noelle sighed. "I actually stopped by to feed your addiction, but also to see if you'd mind taking a drive with me."

Zoe was grateful for the change in the topic. "Where?"

"Don't laugh, but Kade and I are considering buying one of Seth and Asher's houses."

She arched her brows in surprise. "And live in a subdivision? With neighbors butting into your business?"

Noelle pushed back her blond hair as she chuckled. "We thought it might be nice once we have kids. They'd have friends close by, and you know Kade, he enjoys being around people."

Zoe lifted a shoulder and let it drop. "If you say so."

"There's one I really like, but I want your opinion, if you don't mind. I can't decide if there's enough space in the kitchen and if the extra bedrooms are too small. Asher and Seth are done for the day, so you don't have to worry about catching them working."

Zoe glanced at the orange ball sitting low in the sky. "It's going to be dark soon."

"It won't take long. Twenty minutes max, including drive time." Noelle gave her a hopeful look. "Please?"

How could she say no? "Okay. Let me grab my shoes."

Zoe remembered the uneven surfaces of the construction site from the times she'd visited Asher, so she put on a sturdy pair of athletic shoes. Afterward, she followed Noelle outside and climbed into her car.

Several minutes later, Noelle pulled in front of the same house Asher had been working on before. With no other cars or trucks around, a relieved sigh eased out of her. The home looked to be nearly complete. "This one?" she asked Noelle.

"Yeah, it's so pretty, isn't it? Asher and Seth have done a great job."

Zoe looked over the structure, once again admiring Asher's remarkable skills. "It's beautiful."

Noelle beamed. "Twenty percent down, and it's ours. Plus, I'm sure they're giving us a great deal on price."

She smiled, trying to allow happiness for her friend to block her forlorn feelings. "I would hope so. Let's go look."

Zoe pushed open the passenger door of Noelle's vintage Mustang. Instead of the dirt hill that had been in front of the house, someone had smoothed it down and poured a cement driveway. It really would be an adorable home.

They mounted the steps, and Zoe reached for the knob, finding it unlocked. Scents of paint and new carpet greeted them, and she loved the endless possibilities the empty room inspired for decorating.

They'd taken a few steps when Noelle suddenly stopped. "Shoot. I forgot my phone, and I wanted to take pictures. I'll be right back." Noelle hurried out the front door while Zoe continued to look around.

From the corner of her eye, she saw Noelle's red car pull away. She whirled around and rushed to the window to see her friend driving off. Panicked, she ran to the porch and yelled after her, but Noelle kept driving.

"What the hell?"

She pulled her phone from her pocket and dialed Noelle's number. She'd understand if Noelle had received an emergency call, but she didn't need to desert her without a word.

"Zoe?"

The sound of Asher speaking her name stopped her cold. She pushed the end call button on her phone, silently promising she'd make Noelle pay for her treachery.

Slowly, she turned and faced the man who'd stolen her heart. "Asher." God, he looked good. Too good.

"What are you doing here?" he asked.

Her cheeks flamed when she realized he'd been duped as well. "Noelle brought me here. She wanted me to see the house she and Kade were planning to purchase from you."

He frowned. "They're not going to buy this house. We've already sold it to another couple."

"Yes, I've also figured that out...now that she left me here with you."

Understanding brought a smile to his face. "Oh. I see. This is a ploy to bring us together. I wondered why Seth left so quickly."

She couldn't have been more humiliated. She was sure the last thing he wanted was to be stranded with her. "I'm sorry. I don't know what they were thinking. The Carters live maybe a mile from here. I'll walk there and catch a ride home. I'm sure they won't mind. Hopefully, Seth will be back soon."

She turned to extricate herself from the embarrassing situation. She'd thought being teased in grade school was bad, but this was nothing in comparison.

"*Zoe. Wait.*"

She halted as her heart stopped and then restarted. She paused for a moment to steady herself and then looked at him.

He held her gaze. "I'm not sorry this happened."

She lifted her brows, not daring to breathe.

He moved close enough she could see the flecks of silver in his eyes. "I've been wanting to talk to you. In fact, that's probably why Seth arranged this, because he's tired of listening to me saying I'm going to call you."

"Did you change your mind about the house?" She couldn't imagine what else they would need to discuss.

"Yes."

Pain wrapped its gnarly fingers around her throat. She shouldn't have thought he'd meant something else. When would she learn? "Oh...okay. But I think they've completed my paperwork. I could sell the house to you, but I would need the twenty thousand I put down, and not the ten that Jenkins charged you."

After all, Jenkins *had* sold it to him first, and she'd had a hell of a time living there without him. He'd offered her an out, and taking it seemed like a good choice.

Surprise twisted his expression. *"Jenkins asked you for twenty thousand down?"*

She nodded, feeling like an even bigger fool.

He shook his head. "Zoe, I don't want to buy the house from you."

She searched his features in the dying light, trying to understand.

He took her hand, his eyes brimming with sincerity. "I want to *live* in the house *with you*. I want to come *home*, Zoe. If you'll have me."

Her throat closed, refusing to allow any words to escape.

He kissed her fingers and then placed her hand over his heart. "You once said you loved me. Please tell me I haven't ruined that. I was stupid and scared, and it wasn't until I lost you that I realized how very much you mean to me."

"Asher..." Tears welled in her eyes as her heart waved caution flags. "Are you sure?"

"I love you, Zoe. More than the sun, the moon, and the stars could ever hope to. One thing being apart has taught me is that you're my heaven, and I need you in my life. I can't live without you."

It took several moments staring at the love burning in his eyes before she trusted enough to throw her arms around his neck and hold him close.

He laughed and squeezed her tightly. "Does that mean yes?"

She nodded fervently. "Yes, yes, and yes."

He kissed her hard and then pulled back to search her face. "I love you, Zoe. I always have, and I always will. Even if you end up breaking my heart."

She placed her hand on his cheek. "I won't, Asher. I love you too much. Your heart will always be safe with me."

He smiled and pulled her to him once again.

"Do you think if we call and tell them we made up, someone will come get us?" she asked.

A laugh rumbled from deep in his chest. "Probably, but we should let them stew for a while. Let them wonder." He lifted her chin and placed a powerful kiss on her lips. "In the meantime, I know how we can keep busy."

A playful smile curved her lips. "Oh, you do, do you?"

"I do. And it starts like this." He buried his fingers in her hair and tugged, forcing her to look up at him.

She grinned. "You'd better kiss me. And don't try to talk your way out of this one."

He touched a fingertip to her nose. "Trust me, my love. I have no intention of ever talking my way out of anything that has to do with you."

"Good. I'm glad you've finally learned."

"I certainly have." He captured her lips, setting her on fire.

She hoped he knew he'd never need to worry about his heart, for she'd treasure it for the rest of her days.

EPILOGUE

Heavy rain poured as Zoe emerged from her office at City Hall and waited beneath the portico for Noelle. Dark clouds hovered overhead, promising the rain wouldn't dissipate soon. Asher wouldn't be happy about the missed hours at work, but she'd be guaranteed a delicious dinner that night, so she wasn't about to complain.

Her friend arrived a few moments later, running through the rain to deliver her peace offering and plea for forgiveness after leaving her stranded with Asher. Breathless, she held out a white bag.

Zoe chuckled at her antics. "You really didn't need to bring this over. Not in this weather."

Noelle wiped rain from her cheek. "We had a deal. A week's worth of cinnamon rolls and then you could forgive me. This would be day seven, sealing our deal."

Zoe grinned. "You know I love you."

"That's good. I was worried things with Asher wouldn't go well, and you'd hate me forever."

She opened the bag and inhaled deeply. "It was questionable there for a few moments."

Noelle laughed. "I'm glad Asher manned up instead of running away again."

"Me, too."

Zoe narrowed her gaze as Earlene Smith emerged from Andersen's Grocery and opened her umbrella. "No thanks to that gossip monger over there."

Her friend followed her gaze across the street.

"She told Asher I'd retained a lawyer. Can you believe it? There's no way she could have overheard us that day in your shop, could she?"

Noelle narrowed her gaze in thought. "I wouldn't think so, but with her, I never know. She seems to know everything about everybody."

The older woman walked to the corner across from them. There, she stopped and balanced her umbrella as she dug in her purse.

"She's probably headed to my place right now," Noelle said. "I should get back."

Zoe shook her head in disappointment. "Where better than there to hear all the latest?"

Her friend gave her a knowing nod. "But it will bite her in the butt one day. And that day might be today."

Across the street, Earlene had her back to oncoming traffic. Zoe spotted what Noelle must have seen, a big semi coming down the road, splashing a thick spray of water as it went.

"Mrs. Smith!" Noelle yelled, but it was too late.

The big truck passed, leaving a muddy, dripping old lady tossing f-bombs left and right.

Zoe snickered and then laughed.

"Don't make fun of her. It's mean," Noelle said, though she wasn't doing a great job holding back her mirth.

"You know what that was, don't you?" Zoe widened her grin at the thought.

Noelle raised her brows. "That truck?"

She nodded. "The karma bus in disguise. The meddling old woman deserved every bit of what she got."

Her friend snorted. "She absolutely did. Do I think it will change her? No."

"Are you okay?" Noelle hollered across the road, but Mrs. Smith was too busy sputtering and wiping water from her face to answer. "I should go help her."

"You do that," Zoe said. "As for me, I'm going to kick off early today. I've got some pressing matters to attend to."

Interest sparked in her friend's eyes. "Would those pressing matters have anything to do with Asher?"

By the look on Noelle's face, Zoe knew she couldn't lie and get away with it. "As a matter of fact, they do."

Noelle's eyes sparkled with humor. "I should rub it in your face, you know? That I was right about him."

"I'm sure you will." For years to come. But that was all right, as long as she had Asher to hold her every night.

I hope you enjoyed Zoe and Asher's love story. Read on for an excerpt from Breathless, the next in the Aspen Series.

Sign up for my newsletter to receive notifications of new releases, freebies, and special sales at www.CindyStark.com. Also, if you have a moment, I'd appreciate a review!

Thank you very much, and happy reading!
Cindy

PREVIEW: BREATHLESS

1

Laurel Ewing pulled the navy-blue summer sweater over her head and tossed it on the growing pile of discarded clothes on her bed. The fear that she'd find nothing decent to wear deepened.

She should have said no to blind dating. No to *all* dating. Period. "This is pointless."

Afton Searle, best friend extraordinaire, lifted the sweater and held it up for Laurel to inspect again. "I thought it looked fine."

Laurel rolled her eyes. Afton could make anything look good with her long blond tresses and an enviable figure. With her own auburn hair and fair skin, she had to be a little more discerning. "I don't want *fine*. I want classy. Or sexy. Or how about devastatingly hot?"

She'd never been considered beautiful in the past, by herself or by the guys she knew. Tomboy would be a better description, at least until recently.

Afton sucked her tongue. "You're devastatingly hot in anything you wear."

"You can say that," Laurel tossed over her shoulder, not

bothering to look at Afton. "Since you're engaged to a man who adores you."

In fact, the greatest factor in her decision to date for the first time had been her friends' romance. Seeing the happiness Afton had found when she'd fallen in love with the sweet and handsome Corey Kendall left her wanting.

Corey hadn't been another weight in Afton's already heavy load. Instead, he'd helped Afton through some unbearable times, leading Laurel to think she might find a guy to love her like that, too.

Since then, she'd discovered dating wasn't as easy as it looked. Finding someone she might be interested in who was also interested in her had been defeating. "You've forgotten what it's like trudging through the dating swamps, looking for a prince among all the warty, rude, and seriously lacking toads."

Laurel turned and held up a red silk blouse she'd worn only twice. Afton shook her head. "Clashes too much with your hair."

She reined in her frustration and continued the search. There had to be something suitable. "You're not helping."

"Don't worry. You look beautiful just the way you are."

Laurel's irritation slipped out. "Like this? Should I go mostly naked then? Just my bra and panties?"

Afton laughed, bringing a smile to Laurel's face. "You said you wanted to be sexy."

"Seriously, though. I do want to make a good impression. You know what they say about first impressions. And don't give me the crap about if he's the right guy, then he'll love me no matter how I look. He's my first actual date that has potential. A successful entrepreneur."

Her friend grinned. "Don't forget hot. And charming."

Laurel snorted at Afton's description. They both knew she

was looking for someone strong and steady. Handsome was nice, but unnecessary. "If what you say about him is true, I don't want to blow it."

She wanted to find a guy and get out of the dating pool as fast as possible. No telling how many piranhas swam in those dark and dangerous waters.

Afton curved her lips into a reassuring smile. "He's a great guy. Don't worry. Your only concern tonight is if there's any chemistry. If you pass that critical point, you will be perfect for each other."

The guy sounded too good to be true. But if he was half the man Afton promised, she could work with that. She didn't need the perfect guy. Just someone she could count on who wouldn't break her heart. As much as she'd tried to convince herself otherwise, she dreaded the thought of being alone forever.

Laurel emptied her lungs with a slow breath. First dates were stressful enough. Blind dates pushed her boundaries of sanity. She wasn't shy. Hell, she'd interviewed tons of people in search of the perfect news or human-interest story. But add in the potential new love interest factor, and her brain went to mush.

"Let me have a look." Afton stepped in front of her closet and rifled through her clothes. "Wear this one."

Laurel had already decided against the forest green button-down blouse. "That won't work. Too plain."

Afton arched a brow. "That's what accessories are for, my dear. Put it on."

She took it with an exasperated sigh. The fabric was soft and had a slight sheen, making it dressier than a plain cotton shirt. She assessed the blouse with fresh eyes as she buttoned it. The color did look good with her hair. "It's not very sexy."

"Undo an extra button. Show a little cleavage. It's not against the law."

No, but it *was* unnatural for her. She slipped the button out of its hole and gave the shirt another opportunity to impress her. She turned to the side and glanced in the mirror. The darts around the midsection tapered the shirt to her curves, and with the one button undone, it hinted at sexy. Subdued sexy.

Afton pointed toward the dresser. "Finish it with that chunky metal heart necklace you have, and I think we have a winner. Perfect for dinner at Pinecone's finest restaurant."

Laurel didn't meet her friend's gaze, but turned to choose her necklace instead. "We're not going to Pinecone. We decided to stick closer to home and meet at Sparrow's." After a long moment of silence, Laurel glanced at her in the mirror.

Afton pinned her with a knowing gaze. "*We decided*? Or you did?"

She flashed a warning look at her friend. "Does it matter? You know I dread going to Pinecone, and he didn't seem to mind. Plus, if I drive myself, which I wouldn't if we went into Pinecone, I can leave early if things don't work out. Win-win in my book."

Her friend gave her a look that said she was crazy. "If you're both happy with that choice, then I guess that's fine. I would have gone for the nice dinner out of town, but whatever."

Laurel ignored her taunt. "Cowboy boots or heels?"

"I'd go for heels, just to dress it up a bit."

Of course she would. Afton had tried to persuade her she didn't need to dress to impress, but they both knew she did. For now, she convinced herself that the reward would be worth the effort. All she wanted was a decent guy who could be happy with small town living and a normal, quiet life.

Didn't seem like it was too much to ask.

———

Laurel shifted her old yellow Jeep into park and wiped her sweaty hands on her jeans. *Breathe.* Just breathe, for heaven's sake.

Her heart thudded loudly, fueled by a mixture of excitement and nerves. What if he *was* Mr. Right? What if the man of her dreams waited just inside Sparrow's Bar and Grill? Her odds were fifty-fifty.

It *could* happen.

As she headed toward the door, she scanned the parking lot, looking for a vehicle she didn't recognize. Since her date was basically a stranger in her small town, whatever he drove should be easily recognizable. She scanned the half-filled parking lot twice and found nothing out of the ordinary, letting her know he hadn't arrived yet.

That was okay. She had shown up a little early because her nerves demanded it. That didn't make him late.

At least she hoped he wouldn't be. That would mean more time to fret about the evening if he was.

Breathe, Laurel.

Fresh air, thick with the scent of pine, helped to lower her anxiety. The evening was beautiful with the warm summer sun headed toward slumber in the western sky. The heat of the day had passed, promising a beautiful mountain night in its wake.

It was the perfect atmosphere for lovers. Maybe, just maybe, she might meet a man she could love, too.

Sparrow's familiar scents of sizzling steaks and beer greeted her as she entered. Several people acknowledged her with a friendly nod. She returned a brief smile before she shifted her gaze from table to table, looking for a tall guy with dark hair, as Afton had described him. Just in case he'd parked elsewhere.

After checking the front area, she headed toward the back where the loud music mellowed and several guys played pool.

Her date wasn't there, either. Not that she'd expected him to be.

With her nerves skittering just beneath her skin, she claimed an out-of-the-way seat that faced the front of the bar and focused on calming her nerves. Becky, the bartender, took her order and returned with a glass of white wine a few minutes later.

Dating sucked. No doubt about it. The entire process was ridiculous. She shouldn't worry about what he thought of her. Maybe he should try to impress her instead.

Worse, maybe she'd take one look at him and *not* want him to. Then she'd be left to deal with the sticky process of extricating herself from the situation without hurting his ego.

Odds were one of them wouldn't be going home happy tonight. Possibly both. Possibly...

A male voice pulled her from her doomsday reverie. "Hey."

Laurel lifted her gaze with hope rising in her heart, only to have it dashed. Tall, dark, and handsome. One of Corey's friends, if she remembered right. Though she couldn't recall his name. Mostly because she hadn't wanted to remember it.

He was a ladies' man who didn't know how to take no for an answer. At least that's how he'd come across, with his over-the-top flirtations, when she'd briefly met him. And she had no patience for his kind.

She glanced behind him to ensure her date hadn't arrived. The last thing she needed was a good-looking man to scare away her potential soulmate. "Hi."

With midnight eyes and sensuous lips, she could safely assume he'd kicked up plenty of dust on the multitude of broken hearts he'd left as he plowed on to the next.

Which was exactly why she'd blown him off more than a year ago on the night Afton had been unjustly arrested. Laurel never forgot a face. He'd been an outrageous flirt who'd come on far too strong. Knowing how devastating he could be to her, she'd rejected his advances with some well-placed words.

Then everything fell to pieces with Afton's arrest, and she hadn't seen him since. She could have asked Afton's fiancé about him if she'd been interested, but she knew enough to avoid disaster before he could wreak destruction.

He lifted his chin in an assured manner. "Are you going to tell me your name this time?"

Laurel chuckled as her cheeks heated, surprised that he'd remembered their conversation from that long ago. She gave him the save answer she had back then. "No."

Because if she did, he'd ask for her number next. Then, if he actually did call, she wouldn't know what to do.

He shook his head. "Still playing hard to get? Doesn't matter. You'll tell me, eventually."

No, she wouldn't.

She glanced behind him again, worried her date would walk in and see them together. Which would not be a great first impression. "I hate to seem rude, but I'm waiting for someone. A date," she added, just in case he didn't catch the hint.

He arched his brows. "Oh, really? Me, too."

She exhaled with relief. Dangerous player avoided. Score one for her.

He glanced at his watch, and a small frown settled on his expression. "She seems to be running behind. Anyway, nice to see you again."

He gave her a brief nod before he strode away to claim a nearby table, where he could also watch the front door.

She made a face behind his back and then looked away. Who was he dating anyway? Had to be someone from Aspen, or he wouldn't be in her town. Lexie? Or Mallory? She'd bet it was Mallory with her long, dark hair and pretty, blue eyes. She'd be just his type.

Laurel lifted her glass and sipped to avoid the awkwardness of being alone.

Five minutes passed. Then ten. She grew anxious, wondering if her date had stood her up. Mr. Flirt had caught her sneaking glances far too many times, and she feared he'd think she was lying. She'd consumed more than half of the glass of wine she'd ordered, and her evening was on a serious downhill slide.

She heaved a sigh of frustration.

Why did she put herself through this?

Laurel drained the rest of her glass, not wanting to waste the excellent vintage, and stood. Without looking in the flirt's direction, she headed toward the front of the bar. A night at home with the dogs sounded better and better.

"Looks like maybe we've both been ditched," he called out before she got far.

She swiveled on her heels. "Apparently so. That's the last time I let a friend pick a date for me. She promised he was hot, successful, and charming." She might have been bragging, but he deserved it.

His eyebrows shot upward, filling her with satisfaction. "Is that so?" he asked.

Maybe her date had a good reason for not showing, but he could have texted her if he wasn't going to make it. Leaving her hanging was nothing but rude. "That's what I was told, but he seems more like a loser to me. If he thinks I'm waiting any longer, he can think again."

He stood and strode closer before he spoke in a quieter tone. "You're here on a blind date?"

She shrugged, pushing down her embarrassment. "People do that. It's not uncommon." It didn't mean that she couldn't get her own dates. Afton had insisted that she meet her friend.

A devilish grin slid across his lips as he shook his head. Then he laughed. "I can't believe it. I begged Afton for the longest time to give me your number, but she refused."

Laurel gaped at him, thinking there was no way Afton would have hooked them up. Especially not without telling her.

He strode closer, tightening the tension inside her. "Apparently, my persistence wore her down. Though she must know you'll have her head."

If what he said was true, she most certainly would.

ABOUT THE AUTHOR

Award-winning author Cindy Stark lives in a small town shadowed by the Rocky Mountains. She enjoys writing about forever love with hot men and strong women in her sexy contemporary romances, along with penning unexpected twists in her emotional romantic suspense stories, and creating magical mayhem in her paranormal cozy mysteries.

She'd like to think she's the boss of her three adorable and sassy cats, but deep down, she knows she's ruled by kitty overlords. Someday, she hopes to earn enough to open a cat sanctuary where she can save all the kitties and play all day with toe beans and murder mittens.

Connect with her online at
www.CindyStark.com

ALSO BY CINDY STARK

ASPEN SERIES (Small Town Sexy Romance):

Wounded (Prequel)

Relentless

Lawless

Cowboys and Angels

Come Back To Me

Surrender

Reckless

Tempted

Crazy One More Time

I'm With You

Breathless

PINECONE VALLEY (Small Town Sexy Romance):

Love Me Again

Love Me Always

ARGENT SPRINGS (Small Town Sexy Romance):

Whispers

Secrets

BLACKWATER CANYON RANCH (Western Sexy Romance):

Caleb

Oliver

Justin

Piper

Jesse

RETRIBUTION NOVELS (Sexy Romantic Suspense):

Branded

Hunted

Banished

Hijacked

Betrayed

COOKIE CORNER COZY MYSTERIES (PG-Rated Fun):

Cookie Calamity

Haunted Cookies

Cursed Cookies

Conjured Cookies

Killer Cookies

Shadow Cookies

SWEET MOUNTAIN WITCHES COZY MYSTERIES (PG-Rated Fun):

Midlife or Death

For Once in My Midlife

One Midlife to Live

Midlife in the Fast Lane

Midlife of the Party

Such is Midlife

Mysterious Midlife

Love of my Midlife

Merry Midlife

CRYSTAL COVE COZY MYSTERIES (PG-Rated Fun):

Murder and Moonstones

Brews and Bloodstone

Curses and Carnelian

Killer Kyanite

Rumors and Rose Quartz

Hexes and Hematite

TEAS & TEMPTATIONS COZY MYSTERIES (PG-Rated Fun):

Once Wicked

Twice Hexed

Three Times Charmed

Four Warned

The Fifth Curse

It's All Sixes

Spellbound Seven

Elemental Eight

Nefarious Nine

Hijacked Honeymoon

A Witch Without a Spell

Mystical Mayhem

WITCHES OF PORT TOWNSEND (Sexy Paranormal Romance):

Which Witch is Which

Which Witch is Wicked

Which Witch is Wild

Which Witch is Willing

OTHER TITLES:

Sweet Vengeance

<u>Moonlight and Margaritas</u>